Can
You Wave
Bye Bye,
Baby?

Can
You Wave
Bye Bye,
Baby?

stories

ELYSE GASCO

M&S

Canadian Cataloguing in Publication Data

Gasco, Elyse
    Can you wave bye bye baby?

ISBN 0-7710-3297-8

I. Title.

PS8563.A678C36   1999   C813'.54   C99-930012-1
PR9199.3.G35C36   1999

We acknowledge the financial support of the Government of Canada through the Book
Publishing Industry Development Program for our publishing activities. We further
acknowledge the support of the Canada Council for the Arts and the Ontario Arts
Council for our publishing program.

The epigraph from "The Speed of Darkness (VII)" on page vii is taken from *The Speed of
Darkness* by Muriel Rukeyser, published by Random House. Copyright © 1968 by Muriel
Rukeyser. Reprinted by permission of International Creative Management, New York.

The lines by Kahlil Gibran on page 29 are from *The Prophet*, published by Alfred A. Knopf,
New York.

The epigraph from "Morning Song" on page 51 is taken from *Ariel* by Sylvia Plath, published by Faber and Faber Limited. Copyright © 1965 by Ted Hughes. Reprinted by permission of the publisher.

The lyrics on page 169 are from "They Can't Take That Away from Me" by George
Gershwin and Ira Gershwin. Copyright © 1936, 1937 (Renewed 1963, 1964) by George
Gershwin Music & Ira Gershwin Music. All rights reserved. Used by permission of Warner
Bros. Publications U.S. Inc., Miami, FL. 33014.

Text design: Sari Ginsberg
Typeset in Centaur by M&S, Toronto
Printed and bound in Canada

McClelland & Stewart Inc.
The Canadian Publishers
481 University Avenue
Toronto, Ontario
M5G 2E9

1 2 3 4 5   03 02 01 00 99

For Kira, of course, my beginning.
Real, true, and unimaginably original.

And for the one on her way:
Hello, Baby. Welcome.

I bastard mother
Promise you
There are many ways to be born.

— Muriel Rukeyser
"The Speed of Darkness"

CONTENTS

Can
You Wave
Bye Bye,
Baby?

A WELL-IMAGINED LIFE

It's a different time and it's one of those homes for girls, a place for pregnant girls to go away to and have their babies quietly, a convent-type thing where it is hoped that all the hushed holiness will keep the girls from heaving and grunting too loudly. One of those places. You know. You've seen the same movies I have. It's a home for these pregnant unweds and an institution for children with Down's syndrome, a kind of catch-all clubhouse for the lost and stigmatized, for all these wounds received during the passion. What difference does it make what the name of the place is? Something French. Sacre Coeur or Notre Dame de Grâce or something. Somewhere in Quebec. Imagine the Plains of Abraham minus the canons and the general war aura. Then imagine that orphanage in *Oliver*. Now put that orphanage on the Plains of Abraham — lots of green and land stretching out, prop up a cow or two, a wire fence that always needs fixing, and a gardener named Jacques-Louis who likes to rub their pregnant stomachs with his rough, muddy hands, and maybe he's just a little slow, a bit retarded, so the girls can fantasize that he is a violent monster, but when that calf gets caught under the wire fence and the Mother Superior wants to slaughter it, isn't it Jacques-Louis who saves the animal and nurses it back to health? And maybe there's a mangy German shepherd, half blind but steadfast loyal to the Mother Superior to the point where these girls in trouble, these girls with reputations, are starting rumours. The English girls give the place a Native name. They call it Shegoneaway. When they see a new face, bloated and tired, thick waterlogged wrists and ankles, they say: Hello, and welcome to Shegoneaway.

She sits at the edge of the narrow cot, neatly made and covered tautly with a white embroidered blanket, the kind that, if you run your hand over it with your eyes closed, feels like a skin disease, tiny white embroidered circles that pop up like pimples. She is The One. You can tell by the way she plays to the camera, showing only her best side, and plus she has the fullest lips, this makes her oddly lovely and they are always oddly lovely. She crosses her hands over her round stomach, as though she is trying to hide something. She wears mirrored sunglasses and wonders if the nun, a young pudgy virgin with one very yellow big tooth, can see her reflection in them. The nun says something to her in French – are you comfortable – are you a whore to end all whores – and she answers: Yes, thank you. *Oui, merci.* The girl in the bed next to hers is wearing just a flannel blouse, some kind of bed shirt, covered in small pink teddy bears, that might give someone the impression of innocence – if it weren't for the fact that she is nine months' pregnant, just sprawled there waiting for the contractions so she can get on with her life, and she isn't wearing any underwear. The nun glances at the girl and reaches over to pat the bare knee kindly, saying in a heavy-accented English: Not too much longer now. The girl smiles meekly, but when the nun turns away the girl rolls her eyes and grabs her naked crotch in defiance. There are no men around and so she makes the nun the enemy.

There are three floors and a cellar. Do you really need a full description? Can't you accept this fantasy shorthand, you know, like who cares how exactly he climbed the trellis to your bedroom window, so long as he cut your clothes off with his sword without nicking you. Fine. Picture a grand wooden staircase twirling up three floors, and everyone's body sweat is a kind of spicy mahogany tinged with a lemon furniture polish, and there's always a lot of action on the stairs, great pregnant pauses on landings where nuns stop to grip a banister and contemplate God, or girls about to give birth stagger down as though they've been shot, clutching their stomachs, water running down their thighs, their hands accidentally pulling down those small framed photographs of Jesus – crying: Help me, help me. Holyfuckingshit. And the clackity-clack of the social-service woman's pumps, a thin hockey stick with a tuft of greying hair, pressing her clipboard against her flat breasts like a shield. And the young sisters, their electric celibacy giving off sparks as they charge hurriedly up and down the great staircase, their habits flapping against their faces like elephant ears, they are whispering with great excitement and great terror: The Nazis are coming. The Nazis are coming. Can I help it if my only nun reference is *The Sound of Music*?

There's a lot of coughing. On the first floor, nuns roll over and cover their mouths. On the third floor, girls who can't find a comfortable position, girls waiting to give their babies away, cough to pass the time, cough and clear their throats as though they were about to say something. And on the middle floor, the children, locked away by their frightened parents who didn't know what to do with those pale dopey faces – hack and gasp in their sleep just to remind the world that they are there.

She, The One, is lying under the pustular spread, her eyes open wide against memories and second thoughts. Somewhere on the second floor she hears a kind of screaming, an animal yelping, like something caught in a trap that snaps to crush bone. It is only the sound of nightmares escaping through their mouths, and though she tiptoes down the stairs of her heart that is creaking with pity, still, she is afraid. Afraid that they will move her child down to the second floor, afraid that she'll move down to the first, and eventually end up in the cellar, lurking in the stone corners with only her stories. Ooo, says the girl in the bed beside her, the girl she calls The Crotch. Ooo, the Mongies are screaming. She scowls at this girl and wraps her arms around herself like a straitjacket. I will go crazy with these thoughts, she thinks. And so she escapes into prophecy, a solace for a weak spirit. She plots the life of the unborn, returning to these images like a soap opera. You will travel, she says. You will love. You will hate anything made with dill. And while she prays this way, silently moving her lips, the whole child's life unfolding like a great map, impossibly life-size, The Crotch is sobbing: Someone shut those mongoloids up.

●━●━●

He leans forward, resting his hairy arms on the desk. He shifts an Eskimo sculpture, some carving of a walrus and her pup, from one side of the cluttered desk to the other. If I look down, I can see his big feet, in his big suede walking shoes, crossed at the ankles. He waits. I don't know where I got that bit about the mongoloids. I guess I must have read it somewhere. I do know that in high school, a teacher who every day seemed to be losing tufts of his hair (poodle-like curls, strangely apricot coloured) backed me against the lockers and asked if I would see him in his office. He was pale and blotched easily and I was half in love with him, so that for a moment I imagined that something huge was about to happen. Instead, he handed me a small folded pamphlet that said *Re-examining Adoption.* My eyes fixed hard on the word *examine* and my cheeks burned. In his office, he stuck his head out the small cubicle window and smoked a cigarette while I sat on his swivel chair, spinning myself dizzy. The wind whipped at the smoke and I worried for his hair. Any minute now, I thought, he is going to turn around and kiss me, but all he asked was if I would come to his Family Life class and talk about adoption. Just the word itself made me feel slightly seedy, slightly exposed. Sure, I answered, regaining my adolescent form, snappy, bored. No biggie.

To his classroom I wore a short, pleated skirt and sheer blue nylons, and I sat on his desk with my legs crossed. I made jokes. When some of the kids asked if I felt normal, kids who still thought it was funny to stick a pencils up their noses or show you the chewed-up food in their mouths, I made a spazzy face, eyes bulging, mouth gaping, and asked them what they meant. Of course there was this one girl, also adopted, but she wouldn't tell anyone. She just sat there glaring at me with her dark, dark eyes and her jagged bangs slashed across her forehead. Much later we heard that she tried to stab her mother with a corkscrew and ran away with some musician to Whitehorse. But life is filled with stories. Who really knows why anyone disappears?

You see, I grew up thinking that none of this was supposed to make a difference, but all I can seem to do is imagine, and imagine being imagined. I feel *her* talking to me in great imperatives, my favourite tense, so confident and unhesitating. She follows me like a camera. I am always looking over my shoulder, fixing my hair, adjusting my underwear, in case she's watching.

He moves his thumb up and down absently, as though he is pressing a lighter, a leftover habit from another time maybe. He sucks on things, whatever he can find on his desk – a pen cap, an envelope opener, an uncurled paper clip. He has this way of smiling only with his eyes, his mouth stays as a scribbled pencil line across his face, but on command he can make his crows' feet appear. He thinks that it is charming, but it's just a trick, like making your ears wiggle. It's difficult to ignore and it forces you to say something.

I say: I read somewhere that over half of a normal conversation can be heard from inside the womb. I think some psychologists are trying to get women to read to the fetus, to tell it stories, under the notion that it is good for the baby to begin to relate to its environment. This is all very interesting but someone is going to have to define "normal conversation" for me. But the greatest part, the real clincher, is that the fetal ear is so sensitive to noise, so susceptible to your vibrations, that you have to be extra careful, extra soft and gentle with your language – otherwise you could do some real damage.

Underneath his desk he is rocking one big foot back and forth on its heel, like a metronome, or a wave goodbye. He gropes for something to put in his mouth. He starts for the stapler but stops himself in time. Here it comes. You know, he says, reaching for a fountain pen, it's not easy to lose a baby. He is very astute, to know almost instinctively that it is not like a set of misplaced keys, that there are only so many places a baby could hide.

She is timing The Crotch's contractions and someone else has gone to find a nun. She is holding the sweaty girl's hand and the girl is screaming: Get it out of me. Stupid bastard baby. The Crotch is fierce. She wants to sing in nightclubs, she wants to smoke cigarettes, she wants to wear red dresses and be thin again. I don't know if you can tell, she says, her face suddenly relaxed, almost flaccid, but I used to have a really great ass. Finally, when they take The Crotch away, she leans back on her own pillows and pushes her fists hard into her temples. She thinks of The Crotch doing her stripteases, playing with her fat stomach like it's a third breast, she thinks of her lightly playing bongos on her belly, making up those really sorry love songs she thought she'd try out on a few record producers when she started her life over again. That's how she begins all her sentences, all her stories, all her plans: When I start my life over again I will . . . And one day, when a nun was slightly short with her, unusually sour, her habit freshly ironed and stiff, The Crotch said: I'm telling you. Give it to Jews. They know how to laugh at themselves. They're even iffy on the hell thing. And celibacy is not an option. She imagines The Crotch having sex, her mousy hair wet across her forehead, every part of her flexed and arched, fingers and toes, the skin just below her pointy collarbone flushed with patches of red, so completely part of the moment that when she opens her eyes it is as though she has been given a post-hypnotic suggestion: *You won't remember anything* — and she doesn't. She imagines The Crotch giving birth, the same sticky hair clinging to her cheeks, and she thinks: She'll be all right. She will not brood. But in the morning she sees that The Crotch is curled up into a prickly ball, like a hedgehog, and won't speak to anyone.

◉◉◉

Anyway, I'm certainly not the first to hear voices, though I'm not even sure I'd describe it exactly as a voice, more of a presence really, a watching, like voodoo, only you don't need a wax figurine, or a chunk of hair, or a piece of tooth. Think of Moses. Put in the bulrushes as a baby, raised in another woman's house, he suddenly started hearing voices. And when he asked the voice who it was, the voice of Our Father the King, the voice said something like "I am that I am" – like some kind of long-haired bohemian free spirit, an ancient freakish guru. I mean, that's an answer the tightest social-service agency couldn't get away with. I read somewhere that hearing voices was the normal way of making decisions before 1300 B.C.

He has a new habit. Tugging at the little tufts of hair in his ears. His hand begins to caress his cheek, his fingers trace the outline of his bones, and suddenly, quite by surprise, he is delighted to find a wee harvest in his ears, miniature sheaves of wheat. He pulls and twirls, concentrating hard on the strangeness of these new sprouts. His hands always near his ears now, he seems to be blocking my voice. Sometimes he strokes his eyebrows, brushing them in both directions, like suede, all the hair on his face suddenly fascinating to him, his hands shielding his eyes like an awning. Maybe I am glowing.

I have a friend, a psychic. She puts her hands on my head and rubs my hair into little knots. She writes a column in the paper called "Notes from the Other World." She writes things like: *Josie from Poughkeepsie . . . Check the lining of the herring-bone raincoat. Ella of Trois Rivières . . . the woman you buried was not your mother.* She sips a strange tea, a brew of almonds and garlic. I lean back on her pillows, away from her mouth. She shoots geography at me, places I might have come from, looking for the natural features of my terrain, waiting for a reaction, some kind of rash of recognition. Malawi? Minsk? Auckland? You know, she says, I thought I saw your eyes dilate when I said Tonga. She tells me that in the ninth month, eyes are open in the womb. She believes that things live and die because they want to, that we have this much control, that there are layers of knowing, like skin, and you peel and peel but now you've done it — look, you're bleeding. She also believes that in a past life she was the Pharaoh Daughter's foot masseuse. When I tell her that I think I am being followed, she says: Are you sure you're not being lead, a heavy, malleable, dull grey element?

On a summer day, I see a man in a black parka and a thick, wiry beard running down the sidewalk, heading right for me. I move to get out of his way, but he hits me on purpose, a solid shoulder check, and runs right past. I think: That was her. And my arm bruises. The telephone rings in the middle of the day and a voice says: Are you satisfied with your paper service? And I say: It's you, isn't it? A young teacher in Baton Rouge sits in front of her grade-five class and suddenly, in the middle of history, begins to eat her wooden desk. By the time the principal gets there she has eaten one corner clear off, and they say it was a vitamin deficiency, and of course I wonder if that's her.

First there was God. Then we invented the video camera – sometime, smack in the middle of my adolescence – and I was convinced that someone had put one in my bathroom, my bedroom, anywhere that I had to be, anywhere that I had to get undressed. In the bathroom, I pulled down my pants and covered myself with towels, and wiped, front to back, shrouded in terry cloth. If I stripped suddenly and exploded into a kind of erotic modern dance, I'd worry endlessly, worry that this videotape would arrive and there I'd be in a movie of myself doing all the crazy things everyone does behind closed doors but can't admit to until they are old enough to believe that it was all a dream. No sense that this life was my own; it was possible that any minute I'd be caught with my hands in metal cuffs just to see what I'd look like in this sort of position, and somehow none of these secrets was my own. It's like those weird science-fiction stories where privacy is impossible and every woman is every child's mother.

I know he is thinking by the way he twirls a clump of ear hair, by the way he presses his lips together with his fingers into a kind of flat duckbill. And he is rocking, back and forth, nursing his idea. Finally, he speaks. You know, he says. There is in the word *mother*, the word *other*. I am thinking: Yes, and the words *her*, *the*, and *or*. And in the word *assistance*, the word *ass*. But I am prepared for his silliness. This is not the first time we've played word games. I pull out my dictionary and show him another definition for the word *mother*. It says: A slimy film composed of bacteria and yeast cells, active in the production of vinegar. You have to look these things up. You have to be clear on your terms. Otherwise, you'll believe anything. And even here, now, I feel her, she knows I am here, she is telling me that I have to be clear on my terms. I am only a figment.

◉◉◉

She was away and now she is not, and she tells herself that the baby is dead, and sees a certain horrible blueness that makes it all believable. It is still a time of privacy – when windows still have shades and curtains and people pull them down and believe they are secluded, when everyone suspects but nobody knows anything, when diseases are whispered instead of advertised on billboards, when there are still hedges you can peer over, and people save coupons and canned food instead of trees, and she didn't say to herself: Dead? What do you mean by dead? Do you mean lacking sensation, numb? What about without elasticity, complete or utter, perfect or exact? Or do you mean – the coldest, darkest, most intense part – as in, the dead of the night? She sits on the long swing, sheltered by the green plastic awning. She rocks back and forth on the wooden porch, waiting. There are still six more weeks of bleeding. She thinks of The Crotch, silent and curled around herself, making the surface of her smaller, shrinking the places you could touch her, bleeding somewhere by herself. When she opens her eyes in the morning, there it is, that feeling that she has forgotten something, that something has been misplaced, that in another time maybe it was her homework, or a friend's good pearl earrings, or her mother's fancy umbrella. There must have been a time, she thinks, when everything had its place. There are many different types of fantasies. She invents order. She rocks herself back and forth. After creation, it is good to just sit and rest and she is too tired to move. You can have a whole life in your head and never have to go anywhere.

There are many things to think about. This is what she chooses: she arches her head back and shows him her neck. He traces the veins, the feeling of them pumping out, bulging, making her really three-dimensional. His is the first body and even though her eyes are closed, she misses nothing. She measures the width of his chest with her palms, the length of his lips with her baby finger. She lets him in because the music that year is so good and because she believes that the body comes first as an ambassador, an emissary of goodwill and promises of tomorrow.

Who knows who he is? I used to think maybe a great poet or a misunderstood Hell's Angel who died playing chicken with an eighteen-wheeler. Now when I see the way she follows the bump on his nose with her fingertips, the way she moves her hips in calm perfect circles, I see that it was not a desperate vagabond love, but something she really believed would last forever. Her promise ring is thin and simple, and it is this simplicity that is surprising, that she could ever, her, The One, love anyone so ordinary. He folds his clothes, he shaves without a mirror, he wraps his legs around her when they sleep, and in the morning he massages her hands and calves when they cramp. She unrolls her future in front of her like a long red carpet. She paces up and down the aisle, smoothing out the little folds in the fabric, but everything seems to be in order, everything seems as planned – just the way she imagined it. And then one morning he is gone. That's it. Just gone. A small indentation in the bed where he used to sleep, a coffee cup with a film of grinds left in the sink, light-blue underwear neatly balled up in the corner of the bathroom, and a discarded razor blade. And the police shake their heads with pity, their eyes grazing her stomach, but no, she can't be showing yet, and they ask her if she realizes how many people *just literally vanish, poof – and it's like they were never there.* Like little stars exploding, she thinks. Bubble people just popping off into thin air, thousands every day. As though all the forces keeping him together had suddenly been released. Take heart, says one investigator. Matter can neither be created or destroyed. He rolls a cigarette between his thumb and forefinger and tells her that if he's learned one thing it's that these vanished people are always somewhere, *but not necessarily in the form you imagined.*

●●●

He is excited today and cannot get comfortable. He crosses and uncrosses his legs. He leans too far back in his chair and scares himself. He holds his hands under his chin like he's praying. Finally he says: It is not uncommon for adopted girls to give their own first baby up for adoption. It is a syndrome of this legacy. There is no articulate response, nothing the dictionary would cover, so I say: Fucking fascinating. Just fucking fascinating. He says: Yes, tell me about that. So I do.

I seduced my first boy dressed as a cauliflower. I must have thought it was alluring, coming to him like that, in a white cotton lace nightgown, something more appropriate for nursing than anything else. Big puffy white sleeves, a billowing skirt, and lace sprouting from my neck. But underneath – this white stem of a body and I can remember wanting it to hurt, wanting to feel myself changing, but there he was, taut and hairless, some kind of moulting bird flapping against me, and I was saying: I can't feel anything. Please, I don't feel anything. I wanted a ripping, something that might feel like life, and when he tried to pull out, whimpering no, to pull away from this raging blaze, I clawed him to me, forced him back inside with my hips, hissing: Give me something.

In the end, it is only the remembering and the imagining that are important. Moments move too quickly, make up the present. Whatever happens, it's always over with in a second. But you have a choice, and if you wanted to you could haunt yourself so well it would become a religion. My friend the psychic doesn't notice that I am getting fatter every day and tells me that everything happens in my mind before it happens anywhere else. So what if I wasn't wearing that pristine nightgown, so what if there was never such a convent, there are a million ways to tell it, just like a horoscope, eventually I'll be right about something. And I feel her with me wherever I go, I have breathed the inside of her flesh, my face pressed into her blood, and so it's no wonder really that I know that somewhere there she is and she is saying to someone, *I don't know, I feel this presence* – and it is only because here I am, imagining, and thinking: There will be days like these when you will feel this presence, and it is not a gift. Think of it as an inheritance.

He is watching me, his head tilted slightly like a spaniel's. He is looking for marks on me, places I might have hurt myself that he hasn't noticed. He seems tired to me today, and I feel protective of him; he has bits of me now and for my own sake I want to support him. He rubs the back of his neck and closes his eyes for a moment and I am embarrassed because suddenly I know what he must look like sleeping. How many versions of the same life can he possibly listen to? He looks down at his hands. He examines his knuckles and then his palms. Maybe he wants to give me his lifeline, maybe he is giving up, maybe he realizes there is nothing he can do for me. Finally, he clasps his hands together hard and I think I can see the blood in his nails. He says: Eventually, you will find a story you can live with. And he opens his hands again, reading the lines to see if he is right.

YOU HAVE THE BODY

I

YOU MEET YOUR MAN AT the outdoor market. He is standing in front of the fruits, feeling the melons and humming
jazz. He stands there like the horn of plenty – gathering
apples and plums, peaches and grapes, pressing them against
his chest, holding them there with the strength of his chin.
You pluck an apple from his neck and say: I am with child.
He stares at you, not understanding, his mouth hanging open
slightly like a little gash in his face. You wait for your words
to wind their way through him, to wrap and curl into a knot
of meaning. You are patient. You have nine months – give or
take. Meanwhile, you snatch a few cherries and shove them
slyly into your mouth. Your man's arms jerk out suddenly
towards you – to embrace you or to push you away, it is all
unclear – and the fruit tumbles to the ground. Things split

apart. Seeds spill everywhere. The old vendor claps her hands in merriment but makes you pay for the fallen fruit anyway. At home you make a bruised-fruit salad and think up names to call the baby.

Selfish. This is how you feel. And you carry this selfishness around like a passport. Your borders, it seems, are already beginning to expand. Still, the world is vast and unsafe and feels as though it could end at any moment. Your friends tell you that there is no greater gift than the gift of life. They are puffy and romantic people, these friends of yours, and remember their childhoods with a boggy dreaminess that makes you wonder if you were ever actually young. Still, thinking about this gift, you wonder if a card wouldn't be just as nice, or maybe cash. Or maybe you should just give blood, something useful. Because once you give the gift, there is no returning it. It is, in fact, a final sale. And what will you say when this life falls apart, when the springs and doohickeys pop suddenly, pop right off, when the instruction manual frays and tatters, smudges and yellows. You suppose you could always tell this little life that in the end it is the thought that counts.

2

You use strange new words. You are surprised at how many times the word uterus comes up in conversation. And areola. And mother. When you say this word out loud you are surprised at how nasal you sound, as though you are joking or making fun of someone. It is common and then taunting and original. It seems self-explanatory, as though there is something in the sound of it that makes its relationship to everything self-evident, but for you the word has always needed a great deal of explanation. Your own mother, for instance, has never carried a baby to term. This seems impossible, really, as you stand there patting your flat belly with your open palm, for here you are. Surely, you must belong to her; the way you sleep with your arm flung across your eyes, the way you line the crisper of your refrigerator with paper towels and keep the mushrooms in paper bags, the way you clear the plates and begin the dishes even before everyone has finished eating. All these tidy things from your immaculate mother and yet how can she help you now?

You have another mother, one probably not quite as clean, who had an advertiser's uncanny imagination and ability to conceive of the whole thing from beginning to end, but for some reason just couldn't believe in it, just couldn't quite buy the product. What can you do? These mothers haunt you.

You straddle these two women, somehow trying to keep your balance, a foot on each fragile back, reaching up like the top of a human pyramid. You have a sense that you are continuing something, but what it is that you are continuing is anybody's guess, like those strange games where you are asked to supply the noun, or verb or adjective, but you have no idea what the story is about, until it is read aloud to you in the end, and you realize how hysterical it is to have supplied all the inappropriate words. *Ladies and Gentlemen, please buckle your heads and place your lives in the upright position.* Things like that. You want to be a part of a great generation of somethings, but it seems you are a kind of Eve, fiddling with your leafy underpants, lonely and nauseated, willing to pluck at anything for vitamins and reassurance. Really, you feel as though you are too curious for your own good, as though you are starting something up.

3

You are still flexible. You plié and bend your head towards your abdomen. You use your belly button as a megaphone and shout: Are you sure you want to go through with this? Eh? You wait for answers. You wait for signs. You think it should have a choice and you are willing to do whatever it wants. You do not feel at all like a mother; your elbows are still black and rough, you still get dirt underneath your fingernails. Instead, you feel more like a candidate. Your hands shake. You canvass your belly for votes of confidence. It is still too early to tell if you have a body of support.

You could almost forget. Its limbs are more like fins. The eyes are on the side of the head. Your imagination seems watery and strange. You take a lot of warm baths, your head submerged so that just your lips and nose break the surface, as though you were something feeding, and you listen to the sounds of fluid, the whoosh like blood through a vein. You imagine that you are the body of the one who could not keep you. She cannot stand the smell of steaming broccoli. She eats pomegranates, her fingers stained and messy from pulling at the seeds. She sleeps with anyone who asks her, trying to fight fire with fire. Absently, she kneads at her stomach, trying to flatten herself. At other times, you are your mother, and when no one is looking, you ease your fingers into yourself, looking for terrible blood.

Helpful people quote poetry at you. Everyone has something to say. At a dinner party with a Middle Eastern theme you fight to keep your tabouli down. When you refuse a glass of wine, a man with hummus in his moustache recites Kahlil Gibran. You have heard this one before. *Your children are not your children / They are the sons and daughters of Life's longing for itself.* Now you say it so often it becomes like a riddle or a joke. You ask: When are your children not your children? And your man answers: When they are the sons and daughters of life's longing for itself. After a while, like all the best lessons in life, like all the finest words, if you say them too often, if you say them too fast, they begin to make no sense.

Your man is very *que sera*. You can hear him humming to himself: Whatever will be, will be. For some reason though, he has stopped shaving. His beard grows erratically across his face, lurching across his cheeks in fits and starts, leaving small patches of stubbly clear-cut in odd places. You have never seen him quite so hairy and you wonder what he is trying to do. When you sleep beside him at night it feels as though he is incognito. He breathes like a spy, like someone waiting behind a door. You have never felt more alone and you cannot figure out your relationship to anything. Sometimes, when he reaches for you at night, you feel as though you are lying under an assumed name.

This is how you imagine it — when your child takes over the house and holds itself hostage in a bedroom. There you are, standing in front of a closed door, afraid to knock again. Inside, all will be quiet and still, and it will remind you of a different time, a time when the door was softer but just as impenetrable. Whatever is happening in there is happening without you. Every now and then you will hear a gasp and it will shoot through you like a torpedo, like a fist through your heart. And you too will gasp, in reflex, in pure jerky pain. You will stand at the door whispering secret words like a game-show host. You will say: Honey? Sugar? Sweetie pie? And the voice from the room will answer: Things made with glucose. You will laugh and feel relieved. You would throw a pie in your face for this kid. But when you knock again, a voice hits the wood of the door like spit. Go away, it says. And you will want to ask: Where? You will want to ask directions in a world where maps are useless and imprecise. The signs for the distance between each place are all way off.

4

You are haunted by her in her new breezy body, walking somewhere, let's say, through a green park or a field of some tall prickly flowers. Her irresponsible little hips swishing, she moves with the smug jauntiness of a remorseless litterbug. There is no word for the kind of criminal she is; a crook who leaves things behind. Something messy billows behind her. "Hey," you want to shout, grouchy like a park attendant spearing the ground, picking up garbage. "Hey, you can't just leave that there."

People tell you that now you will be complete. This makes you wonder what they thought of you before. Incomplete, obviously. An unfinished course, hanging somewhere between passing and failure. It is true that often you feel as though you are missing some essential elements, some crucial parts. "Let's face it," says a girl you have only pretended to like, your man's ex-lover, who is eccentric enough to still be his friend and is regarded as well developed. "Before this, you were pretty childish." "I was?" you ask. And for some reason you want to stick your fingers in your nose. Everyone smells. Some seem to be smugly taking bets on what kind of a mother you will be. You are drawn to these grumps. You peer over their shoulders looking for a tip, trying to figure out what the odds are. You begin to count the number of times someone says to you: I just can't imagine you as . . . well anyway. Still others are even less fun. They are blunt but mysterious. They say simply: Into this world? Aghast, as though they knew another, better, place and if you waited long enough they might reveal this choice travel destination, this exclusive sunshine spot. For fun, you divide these friends of yours into two groups. Those who pronounce fertile so that it rhymes with servile. And those who say it just like turtle. You appreciate the latter. These people seem to have a sense of humour. And you have a strong affinity for this slow reptile; its horny toothless beak, and its soft, stout body enclosed within a shell.

You wake your man in the middle of the night. You say: Quick. When are your children not your children? He is not easy to wake up. He grinds his teeth as though he is chewing something and you can tell that in the future you will be up many nights alone. He mumbles something strange and garbled. You hear: Slums and slaughters. You are losing the poem. Like you, it is growing slippery and changing shape. You lie there getting the words wrong, trying to make sense. Everything seems to be on the tip of your tongue and maybe that is why you cannot speak. You think: They are the slums and slaughters of life's lunging for your neck. They are the guns and plotters. They are the sins and robbers. They will steal your heart away.

It is not at all like having a cat. Your cat is always your cat; there aren't many changes in this relationship. You both might vary your favourite resting spots, your desires for certain foods might wax and wane, but still it is all one long continuum, neither of you ever really interrupting each other, few surprises – old age, death. That kind of thing. Plus, he is neutered. This is something completely different. You could be blamed. In your dreams you are given a choice. You can be Mary, Mother of God, or you can be Dr. Frankenstein. Select now.

Lying with the cat across your stomach, this is what you imagine: you will give the son a Barbie doll. You will try to introduce him to his feminine side. It will be an awkward first meeting. But hopefully soon he will develop and sprout like a proper theory. With loopholes. Because eventually you will have to let him out of the house. Like tropism, he will bend and grow towards the light of the outside, which at times can look eerily like the glow of the television set. He will come home, aim Barbie at your head and say: Pow-pow, mommy. One day you will catch him prying open the legs of the doll, saying: C'mon. Show Ken what you got, hon. What will you do? You will do the best you can. You will teach him about foreplay. You will put condoms in his lunch pail, hidden between the Twinkies and the trail mix.

5

What can you say about your man, except that you are no longer sure that you trust him. He smells like that strange papaya shampoo. He cooks things in the kitchen, shrimps and weird sauces that he knows you can't eat, that make you gag. Sometimes when he lies in front of the television, his mouth hanging open a little, his shirt unbuttoned to his waist, you think: God Almighty, I have made a tragic mistake. I have mated badly. Shouldn't he be preening? Shouldn't he be trying to impress you, carrying sharp twigs in his mouth, swinging from the tallest tree, patting down the earth, stomping and bellowing, ready to protect you from anything? You have always been torn between love and solitude and you think that now you might be crowding yourself right out of your life. When he persists in asking you what you want to eat, you wonder how he ever got into your house. Just what part does he think he actually played in this whole thing? Sometimes when he sees you reach into your pants fearfully checking for drops of blood, he takes it as a sign of lust. You are so wrapped up in your biology it is difficult to understand just what it is that he is doing. Lying underneath him, your whole body groping towards some unimaginable destiny, you say: You know, there is a vas deferens between us. But he does not understand himself enough to get it.

You are surprised when the doctor says that everything is progressing normally. You do not think that you have a history of progressing normally. In your medical file under Family History you have a lot of question marks. You do not know your disease ancestry. You do not know how your mother's labour went, except that here you are. The nurse gives you a few pamphlets to take home and read, brochures, you like to call them, flashy and colourful, like something you might get at a car dealership for something you should decide on with a test drive. Inside one of them you read: *Now you might become curious about your own mother's pregnancies and deliveries.* And you think that this is true. You might.

You imagine her alone. What did this woman know about love anyway? She wore her jeans until they bulged. She drank in dark bars and fell over into the laps of strangers. One night she went home with a piano player and she didn't even wince when he squeezed her swollen breasts. She was flippant with her proteins, fast and loose with her calcium supplements. It's a wonder you are even alive. Is it possible to fill every second of the day so that you never have a moment to think? Once, your mother told you, "I seem to remember something about her being a nurse." A nurse? A fluffy do-gooder student with a fat ponytail and a delicate bedpan manner – gone bad. A defeated caregiver who failed at nursing, whose uniform pulled and gaped in disgrace, whose ankles swelled in her thick white shoes. A crazy woman in her protective mask, switching around the babies in the nursery. Maybe she loved a doctor, an orderly, a patient who died. Maybe some heartless resident promised

her a house in the country and then left her for a cardiol-
ogist. Your mother sends you recipes in the mail for high-
protein shakes, and an article about soya beans. She
highlights all the important food groups and suggests fresh
ginger for nausea and it is then you realize that she has
always known how to take care of you.

You go for your first ultrasound. In the hospital you find
yourself staring at the nurses. Most of them wear glasses and
seem withdrawn. When the technician rolls the probe across
your stomach you realize that you are watching her instead
of the screen. This is a habit you picked up from contemplating the stewardesses on airplanes, convinced that they will
be the first to register signs of impending danger, disaster.
Who knows what you are making in there, what strange
materials you are actually made of. You wait for the technician's facial expressions to change, but she just seems bored.
She does not seem like a good caregiver. She begins to read
out the parts like a merchandise list. Finally, you glance at the
screen and there it is, unbelievably yawning and raising a
small hand in a kind of salute. Your man grabs your hand in
a sudden rush of disbelief and implication. Oh, the things
that grow out of the murkiest longings. The technician asks
if you have any questions. You say: Ask if it wants to be born.
Finally the woman laughs a little and says: Everything wants

to be born. It is the urge to life. Really? you say. Because you desperately want to believe this person who has pronounced your centre alive and well, and you have always had such a hard time summoning up your own eagerness, your own importunity. You are possessed by a strange knowledge, like the realization that most of the dust in your house is actually your own skin. Everywhere you go you leave pieces of yourself. This is an awesome responsibility. You want so badly to believe in the impulse to life, but you remember high school, the horror of those young, urgent lives, grown-up and edgy, and suddenly you feel sick and guilty.

How could you not have noticed before all the pregnant women, all the children on the street, all products of a mounting desire, however brief, however fleeting. You are like someone back from the moon, bewildered by station wagons and family vans, by car pools and video games. What does any of that have to do with what you just saw? You and your man walk home like the first people on earth. You want to take off your shoes and go barefoot. You want to lie face down in the soil somewhere, to smell something real, to plant yourself and grow bushy and full of yourself, like human nature. How can you not feel like a kind of Eve? How can you not want to know everything?

When your child is at school you will memorize encyclopedias. You will read the Trivial Pursuit cards in the bathroom. You will keep the *Book of Lists* under your mattress like an erotic magazine. You will blush with useless knowledge. Secretly you will relearn how to multiply fractions. At dinner one night you might be feeling particularly confident. You will risk everything then. You will say: Go ahead. Ask me anything. I dare you. And your daughter will reach into her chest, pull out her heart and spread it across the table like a royal flush. She will murmur: Look. Who are you? Why does it hurt? All this will stun and frighten you and so you will tell her that the Virginian opossum has as many as seventeen teats. You will tell her that Julius Robert Oppenheimer's main aim was the peaceful use of nuclear power. You will tell her that the atmosphere not only provides us with oxygen, it also protects us from the sun's harmful radiation and the excesses of cold and heat. You will tell her that some people think aliens built Stonehenge. And you will remind her that the peculiar thing about fractions is that when you multiply them, no matter how fruitfully and with what attention, you always end up with less then you expected.

6

Your mother sends you a baby picture of yourself at three weeks, your head still a little misshapen from the inside of some other woman's body, the tremblings of her faithless muscles. You have never been all that gentle with yourself, but for the first time you want to reach out, pick yourself up, and stroke your splotchy newborn forehead. You have a hard time giving anything away, even an old pair of shoes. Spiders rule your bathroom. When a plant dies you never really know what to do with its body, its dusty and crackled-earthy remains. When a cat followed you home, ugly with an eye infection, you cried, but you kept him. Your mother writes that you should send her pictures of yourself, of your ampleness, your unfurling belly button like a pig's nose. But you are embarrassed. Not only by your plain and palpable lust, but by something even more unexpected – your natural and painless fecundity. "I am fecund," you say to your mirrored reflection, and you feel suddenly dangerous and gritty, as though somehow the very term has all the innuendos of a dirty word. You cannot send this image of yourself to your mother, in the bulging costume of a braggart, the grotesque adornment of a betrayer. A strange riddle twists through you with the power and intention of a snake. When is your mother not your mother?

You watch a television show about population growth. A science-fiction writer gloomily suggests that women should just stop having babies for a while, to give the earth time to heal and repair. He says you have to be careful. He says that soon there will be no more room left on the planet. He says we will all die of thirst or claustrophobia. You are so easy to blame. Your shirts do not button properly. You are slow and often dreamy. You whistle for no reason and cry unexpectedly. The TV flashes pictures of dying children, of orphans waiting to be adopted, their legs skinny and bowed, their tiny ribs like washboards. And you think: Oh, pretty please. Just this one. There must be just a little space for this one. Still, you cannot know what you are about to set free and unmuzzled into this world.

7

Spring comes early. Birds lean up against your window like buskers, like colourful folk singers whistling through the screen. It is not strange to you at all that you have timed it to the month of your own birth. You think of life and all its repeating demands. How could anyone have ever thought the world was flat? It is so obviously round, circling over and over again. All the movements inside remind you of live fish held in a plastic bag, creatures you could fool yourself into thinking required the minimal amount of care. Sometimes you imagine that it cannot breathe, that you yourself are made of plastic, artificial and smothering. For both of you there is finally only one way out. You picture the way you must have bruised her inside, or lodged a heel right under a rib, or pressed yourself hard into her bladder or a kidney, forcing her to remember you there. You waited with her like a prisoner, though it is difficult to tell just who was holding who hostage. Clearly she must have gotten the poem wrong, misheard it somehow in a very crowded room so that she could have turned to you and said in all seriousness, in the voice of a poet: Don't you know you are not my child?

8

You are heavy and at times this feels only indulgent. Everyone can see what you are up to. Standing, stretching, anything erect, really, is not as much fun as it used to be. All you want to do is squat. Life moves vigorously now and sometimes when you look down at yourself you can see your own shirt actually moving, fleeting jabs and undulations. When this happens in public you feel like a suspect, a shoplifter, someone whose thievery and hunger is so painfully obvious.

Lately you cannot imagine being loved. You do not know what you will ever do to deserve it. You stay up late eating cheese popcorn and watching terrible movies. Every night it seems there is something on about the invasion of aliens, rubbery things looking for a new home, lodging in people's faces or taking over their lawn mowers. You watch these sad, awful creatures covered in phlegm or mucous as though they've been crying way too long, battling all of life, and you think: Let them be sons and daughters. Let them be songs and drifters. Just let them be. It seems you cannot stop checking the clock or flipping through the pages of your datebook. Suddenly it feels as though you have run out of time to change the world. You decide that if the one inside you needs to burrow into some part of your face or to take over a favourite appliance, you will let it. When you do finally fall asleep, this is what you dream:

One day the child will wake up with a strange glint in the eye, a tiny grimace like a smudge in the crook of the mouth. But when you lick your finger and go to wipe it off, it will be indelible. The child will watch you suspiciously, the way you watch someone blowing up a balloon – waiting for the bust. The child will stalk you warily around the house, and the look will remind you of a time when people used to pick up your hand and say in amazement, "Look at this tiny wrist. I could break it like that." In the child's eyes is a strange brew of disgust and pity and you will see that this child is afraid of becoming you. The child will develop a cruel interest in your life, following you around the house like the paparazzi, asking cunning and subtle questions like: "At what point exactly do you think your life went wrong?" And: "When did you finally let go of your dreams to settle for this?" And you will know that there is no such thing as planned parenthood. All the things you will do right will be by mistake.

In the last weeks you imagine that there is another choice. You are as cranky and unpredictable as a cat. You just want to go off somewhere alone. You know it isn't his fault, but lately when you look at your man, just the sight of him makes you feel like complaining. You imagine that you would be better off on your own where nothing horrible could come out of your mouth. He cannot get his arms around you any more and it feels as though the sheer size of you is already pushing him away. Is it ever possible to get close without really contorting? When he sleeps, peaceful and oblivious, you watch him and think: Idiotic. Nightly, you plan your escape. Two steps to the bedroom door. Twenty-one steps down the hall to the front door. You see yourself behind the wheel of your car, the windows wide open, your hair tangling into thick clumps. Suddenly, the whole world is there, waiting. What do you want? Ocean? Desert? The cold, dark mountains? The road ahead is flat and inviting. Soon, you will be skinny again. You will only wear dresses. You will never be afraid of strangers. You will drink men under the table and sleep with college freshmen. They will read to you excitedly from their textbooks, their cheeks still raw from shaving too fast. You will take a woman lover and live in North Africa with a turban wrapped around your head. There are many sleepless nights like these and you watch your room getting lighter, like tanned skin being peeled back to reveal the pale below. You think that this is like death in the way it makes you want to tidy, to put your affairs in order. You remember all the boys you've slept with and rate them one to ten. Could this really be the last one? You rub your stomach, gently poking at the tiny heel you feel pressing just below your ribs and you wonder: Whose body are we?

9

It happens in a rage. In the beginning it does not seem quite so overwhelming, and you are overcome by shyness. A nurse, her hair pulled back into a tight braid, takes your blood pressure. She smells like rubbing alcohol and peppermint gum and you try to win her over by controlling your facial expressions. Maybe, with enough effort, you will appear neutral and serene. Maybe you can keep all your grunts and animal belling to yourself. You want to show her that you will be no trouble at all. You say: Maybe I could just do this with my underwear on? She gives you a world-weary smile and pats your hand. Her nails are short and clean and filed square. In the end, though, there is nothing demure about life. Instead you find that you have ripped the hospital gown from your body. Your man seems amused but beaten and you cannot bear for him to touch you. Later he will tell you that all you kept shouting was *out*, but he could not believe that you were actually talking to him. You stare into the eyes of the nurse beside you. She seems strong and encouraging. This thing is a battle and until now, you could not conceive of how much you must have hurt her, the scars you left on the woman who left you behind. When they deliver the small blue girl onto your stomach, you are amazed that something so tiny could be so resolute, so earnest. They lift her to you and for one moment you imagine not taking her in your arms, closing your eyes, politely refusing her as though she were a festive party offering, a decadent loot bag or a fancy canapé you might politely decline with a simple *No thank you. Not tonight. Watching my weight. Oh, I couldn't possibly.* Her eyes are a liquid steel colour and she holds your stare easily while you trace her stringy veins with your fingertips; your powerful blood, her iron will. It seems this child will never not be your child. Whatever were you thinking? It is impossible to be this other woman's exhausted body now, her damp sad belly, her sticky hair, her dry bitten lips. They tag your daughter's wrist and you will follow her forever like a wildlife biologist. You hope that someday she will learn to forgive you.

The nurse squeezes your shoulder and quickly turns to leave. She will not turn around again, and you see that she is the one with the braid and that it is coming undone in what seems to you like a kind of abandonment, held together by just a plain rubber elastic. She has left the baby swaddled beside you in the crook of your arm, in your lawless hands that would steal anything for this girl. The nurse makes a sound, a laugh, a tired sigh, something breathy, and pushes the door open with her strong shoulder. She is leaving you alone with this child. She does not tell you that she will be back. Her white coat billows a little like the sail of a small boat surprised by the wind — goodbye, goodbye. You watch her leave and wonder: Wait. Where are you going?

ELEMENTS

Love set you going like a fat gold watch.
The midwife slapped your footsoles, and your bald cry
Took its place among the elements.

— *Sylvia Plath*
"Morning Song"

FIRST OF ALL, WE are not taught to grieve. It is all improv and ad lib, lines coming in where they shouldn't and scenes changing suddenly because no one knows how to play it. Hugging at the cemetery — we only press against each other to hear another heart beat. You prepare for your mother's death all your life, still, it takes you by surprise, it takes you by force, like the savage troubadour of your fantasies. The sky does nothing special. It just hangs there coolly, like a rubber-necking voyeur. It is not yet summer but the trees are just too lush and full of themselves. You turn back to your life, a little more forgetful, and say: Now, where was I?

Understand that it is only your imagination, something about grief and sorrow, and the way the earth smelled when you watered the spider plant, that makes her turn up at your back door and announce after all these years that she is your mother. She says: Finally, after all these years, I am your mother. Eye her suspiciously and think that structurally there is something the matter with her declaration, an insincerity in the grammar that makes you mistrust her. Of course, she is the ghost of the one who gave you away so many years ago and she mills around on your wooden porch like some Shakespearean messenger or lowly spear carrier, waiting for some kind of reaction. Notice that she is dressed in shades of umber and ochre. She has the musky aura of a traveller or a poet. She fidgets with a tassel of her scarf, something with zebras or jujubes, and you stare over her head at your garden that all of a sudden seems to be dying. You mumble, Nothing is perking, and invite her in. Offer her coffee or popcorn – something that takes time, that needs to be made with a machine. While you are melting the butter over a low flame, feeling like an alchemist, looking for original matter, looking for what was originally the matter, you hear many voices. The television is playing and someone is telling the talk-show audience that a healthy fantasy life can lead to all kinds of ecstasy. She stands in your kitchen eating buttered popcorn, the line of grease below her lips making her seem shiny and plastic. She picks a kernel from her tooth and says: I don't know what to ask you. You watch as she picks up a sponge and starts to wipe the top of your fridge, examining the dust after every stroke, and you say: Ask me if I've had a good life. She stops her cleaning, already now bent down near the corners of the stove and on her hands and knees, and she asks: Have you had a good life? You close your eyes and say: I don't believe you. I just don't believe you. You look down at your finger-nails and notice the crescents of earth under your nails and wonder what you've been digging at.

●━●━●

You spend your nights solving for *x*. You are taking College Algebra and Functions, and Introduction to Chemistry, and you spend a lot of time squeezing your hands in frustration. You are starting over again, a jump-started engine that really wants to go somewhere. You want to go to medical school. You want to save people. Sometimes you fantasize about starting a cult. You have lived in your head too long. Now you want to live somewhere else. In a hospital, maybe. With real people, hopefully. Your husband, the veterinarian, tutors you at night. He rolls up his sleeves and, smelling like an animal, like something rich with oily fur, he says: Can't you see? You have to find the root. You wonder if this is the reason for the mud under your nails.

You can hear your daughter humming in another room like something about to explode, a firecracker or a planet. She is seven and she loves her father with a fierce, tooth-bared love that makes you worry for her lovers. She is watching a nature show. You know because you can hear things like: *Over time it will have to change or disappear.* Or: *The dotty-backs live peacefully under the poisonous tentacles of the sea anemone.* Soon she wiggles onto your lap while you are cross-multiplying, and says: Mommy, your blue-green titties are sagging. You try to take her seriously. You read somewhere that it is dangerous to dismiss the observations of little girls. It could lead to loss of self-esteem or the inability to reduce fractions to their lowest common denominator. Really? you say. What should I do? She reaches out to squeeze a breast and explains logically: Put on your algae bra. Suddenly she gets up on your desk and horrifies you as she begins to shimmy a wildly provocative belly dance, screaming: Algae bra and fuck shins. Algae bra and fuck shins. And then she is gone, doing a clumsy Charleston out the door.

Your husband, the one who smells like a retriever, laughs at her dirty jokes and you wonder if he has enough human contact. Say: My mother was here today. She was in our kitchen. I made her popcorn. Your husband tells you that many pet owners who have recently lost their animals swear they hear the ghostly ding-a-ling of a dog collar when the doorbell rings. You want to believe in medicine. You want to believe in him, to grow old and call him Doc. You watch his surgeon hands fiddling nervously with the calculator, plussing, minussing, and clearing, and you know his hands can heal you. Say: Yeah, that must be it, Doc. And he shows you how to write "hell" on the calculator with two ones, a three, and a four. In the other room you can hear your daughter explaining to the cat that some algae are the simplest orgasms known to man.

In chemistry class your professor tells you that everything is made up of atoms. He strokes his bald head and tells you that there are more atoms in your strawberry-flavoured eraser than there are stars in the universe. When you raise your hand and tell him that you're not sure that you believe him, he rubs his scalp a little harder, and in a cracked, betrayed voice, asks to see you after class.

◄●●●►

Your days fill out like forms, where questions like permanent address and local address confuse you. Sometimes you examine each leaf of the philodendron for signs of disease. Sometimes you read your husband's Veterinary Emergency Care book. You read the section on poisons while the oven self-cleans. Things surprise you. For instance, it is okay to eat an Etch-A-Sketch, but it is not okay to drink Head and Shoulders. Usually you hum to yourself, a kind of white noise that keeps time with the refrigerator. Sometimes when you stop humming she shows up, shows up as though your life were a musical and now she has a line. She dresses like Fall, a lot of reds and oranges, sometimes brown; otherwise she seems relatively normal, the way all relatives can seem at certain moments. She tells you that she's a poet and sweeps her hands around in a way that makes you believe her. Each time she appears she seems younger to you, though you couldn't say how. She likes talk shows. She says they give her ideas. When she says "ideas," her eyes roll back a little and she appears possessed or creative. While you do your algebra, adding negative numbers, she eats popcorn on the couch and watches talk shows – gory, historical exposés of women who gave themselves abortions in highway motels with wire hangers or celery stalks. She slides her finger along the inside of the bowl and licks the salt. She says: Don't look at me. I gave you life.

◦◦◦

Your daughter has been watching *Geraldo*. While you are standing in your garden, absently stroking a lupine, she appears at your hip like a cane and says: Is it true that adopted children grow up and kill their parents? You don't know what to say. You can only offer her examples. Say: I didn't – and watch how bravely she kneels in the earth to pull at a worm. You see the angles of her golden back poking through the gauzy undershirt like little bird bones or grasshopper wings, and you know that it is like voodoo, this connection. You can feel the strain on her knees as she bends, you can feel the earth drying on her fingertips – she is the only blood you've ever known – sometimes you think you can hear her veins thumping and it makes your head spin. You can see the wrinkles on her forehead arching and falling like little waves and you know she is thinking. Wonder if you should reassure her. Wonder if you should tell her that you will never give her away. Wonder if you should show her the silvery stretch marks as proof of her birth, your body's own certificate. She stands suddenly, the worm hanging back over her hand in something like a swoon, and you brace yourself against your own waterfall of protection. Whatever it is, you think, whatever she needs, I will go over in the barrel with her. She looks sternly at you and says: I just want you to know that no matter how badly I need the money, I will never kill you. She pockets the worm and marches resolutely into the house.

On weekends you bring your daughter to the clinic so she can watch and admire her father. She looks at his lab coat, splotchy with iodine, and asks, always, every time: Is that blood, dad. Is it? Sometimes you even help hold an animal down, gripping its head in a wrestling embrace to keep it from arching back and snapping off your man's face. Your daughter roams the back of the hospital like an army nurse, whispering *hush now* and *there there* to her wounded soldiers behind the bars. She calls them her guys and lets them lick her fingers. She wants to be renamed Darwin or Noah, she hasn't decided. She is only seven and yet she talks of going to Africa and being adopted by the elephants. Because you are in the habit of taking her seriously, at these moments you flutter your eyelashes against her cheek like a frantic moth and say: But I'll miss you. Like a true evolutionist, she raises your chin in her hands and says: Over time, mommy, you will have to change or disappear. Sometimes you wait patiently, anonymously in the reception so that you can listen to the sound of your husband's voice, which still thrills and amazes you, when he opens up the consultation door and calls: Mel "the Molester" Flanders? Or – Stinky Mulligan? This man, this same man whose voice you know can crack in a rasp of *oh god, yes*, can stand in front of you and say: Send in Count Basset Hound Saltzman.

Your father calls and says: I think there's something the matter with her garden. Too many bugs with too many legs and way too much drooping. What's fabric softener for? Did you know she made the semi-finals in the girls' junior basketball?

The next time she appears you are doing something with sprouts, filling and emptying pita pockets, some sort of nursery chant spinning through your head — how much alfalfa can a pita pocket pocket? You thought you were making lunch but instead it has become an experiment. College Algebra and Functions has made you believe in the possibility of an equation, in the inevitability of a solution. It is electrical. All you have to do is plug in the formula and solve for x. Who knew life was so, well, mathematical. Who knew that there were actual real answers to so many problems. The train problem from elementary school no longer torments you. If a train leaves Port Hope at nine o'clock travelling at a speed of 100 kilometres per hour and another leaves Fairland at ten-fifteen travelling at a speed of 150 kilometres per hour, at what time will the second train overtake the first? You always believed that, no matter what, it all had to do with whether or not the engineer had a satisfactory marriage or whether or not he was heading towards home or away from home. You never believed that all things could be equal. What kind of world did these trains live in? Now, you are beginning to realize that some of that is irrelevant. If you want, things can be neater. There is an answer – so long as you don't question it too much.

Again she is sprawled out on the couch, watching a program called, threateningly, *You Can Too Paint!* A cowboy with a bad scar across his nose and cheek is teaching folks at home how to paint. Each week a different painting. Each week, across the country, people are creating the exact same painting. He tells you which brushes to use and which specific strokes, while the colours of the day flash across the screen. Floral Pink. Misty Grey. Burnt Sienna. He is wearing a cowboy hat and cowboy boots with thick block heels. The camera spends a lot of time examining his boots. Accidentally, across the country, confused viewers are painting his boots in Soft Floral Apricot. Shooey, says the cowboy. Shooey, today we'll be painting chrysanthemums. You turn to the woman you've invented and dressed in baggy print harem pants and a white silk mock-turtleneck. Say: Why is it that all you do is sit here watching this stupid television all day long? Huh? Why is it? She doesn't look at you when she says: So I don't have to talk to you. The cowboy is saying: Today we are painting beautiful mums and when you see how easy it is, you'll be wanting to paint mums all day long. You look over at the woman with the neat bangs and Afghan earrings, the one who could not take care of you and gave you away, and you wonder what it would be like to scribble across her face with Brilliant Vermilion #2. Remember, says the cowboy. Free and easy mums, that's what we want. Shooey.

●—●—●

You bend over your mother's grave like a branch, your fingers reaching like twigs to touch something, but there really isn't anything to touch. You have seen too many films with grave-yard scenes, too much imitation grieving, a few too many still lives with headstones, and you feel as though you are mim-icking sorrow behind her back. There is nothing here, no stones or marble. It is still fresh, like a wound, a great gash in the earth that needs time and air to harden. Someone should explain to you how all over the world people's sutures are opening up, great gaping sadnesses that heal like skin. All your life is spent losing things – mittens, diaries, a fine designer umbrella, hair and skin – things just drop away from you, parachute away to safety. Every few months or so, your bones turn over, replacing themselves cell by cell. The shin you bruised in April is not the same shin sinking into this muddy plot. You whisper a kind of croupy lullaby – *hush now* – and reassure her, like a lover, that she is the only one.

Your chemistry professor attempts a toupee and tells you that in the world there are 112 known elements. Everything is made up of these elements. Some we even share with the dead. Things like this dazzle you. There are more ways to imagine anything than there are elements. There are more various ways to die than there are elements. There are more words in the dictionary, more definitions of the good life, than there are elements. We share something with everything, just in different doses and gazillions of combinations. It is very basic but it is so neat and organized that it blows your socks off. Your socks are made up of carbon, hydrogen, and oxygen.

Late at night you wake longing for a bath. You can feel yourself hardening like clay and you ache for water, any drop of moisture so that you'll feel soft, so that maybe you can be shaped again, maybe you can be changed, is there any way in the world to be changed anymore? Your sleep is filled with voices. You open your eyes saying: What? What was that? You think you can hear your mother's voice like a radio in another room, so low you can barely make out the words, but the tune seems familiar. She is not telling you anything useful any more. If you awake gasping, images from sleep leave a residue and the sheets feel gritty. In your dreams, you are sitting with your mother somewhere outside, eating steamed hot dogs with onions and sauerkraut. You watch her eat slowly, catching bits of onion that fall like pearls into her cupped hands, and your face feels baggy and ugly with worry. It's all right, says your mother. I have breath mints and chewing gum. You want to laugh. God, you want to laugh with her again, and if you never did you want to start. The way she says "chewing gum," it is so girlish, so Audrey Hepburn in ballerina flats, you could cry, you could cry and dance with her all at the same time. You watch her suck the mustard off her fingertips and you say: I miss you. She gets up suddenly and starts to walk away. Pigeons scatter around her. Oh, I know, she answers grimly. When I was alive I missed you too.

Your husband finds you in the kitchen late at night making shoestring french fries from scratch, something your mother used to make, the oil seeping into everything in the house so that for days afterwards everyone smelled slightly fried. What are you doing? he asks, his eyes scary and unfocused without his glasses, his tousled hair spiked up around his head like a crown. You say: I am smoking out the spirits. In case you hadn't noticed this house is filled with ghosts. Peevish, cranky, smart-alecky ghosts. It is way past midnight and you sit at the kitchen table eating french fries coated in so much salt that your lips dry up and pucker and in the morning they are sore and cracked.

Your father calls. I miss her, he says. I can't find the herring. I can't find my thermal socks. What should I do with all her shoes?

Your husband, the one who knows about anal glands, believes in pheromones, and you can hear him sniffing before you feel his hands start to pet you. Let me smell you, he says, and he finds all the creases and crevices of your body, places that you wash only by accident. Lately you ask him if he thinks you're normal. He thinks you are joking. He feels your nose, tells you it's moist, and suggests a diet change. When he sees your lips begin to twitter, he tells you of an old lover who used to get drunk and beg him to bury her in the front garden. He tells you the closest he ever got was playfully lobbing a mud nugget at the back of her head. No, really, you say. Really. Am I all right?

Some things are greater and less than x. This is what you are learning. You are a mature student and you do all the assignments. You are the oldest in your class, the most patient, mysteriously, the most organized. You bring your own mug to class. Your daughter bought it for you and it says MOM. YOU'RE #1 in bold red letters. When you sip your tea or punch neat holes in the handouts, you realize that the other students are probably imagining you having sex. You do not snort or roll your eyes at the professor. But you would like to. It seems as though you have run out of time to be gangly and bored.

◉◉◉

She seems younger to you, less dense somehow, as though her molecules were moving farther and farther apart. It is an odd youngness, wispy, something you could walk through. She stands at the fridge drinking out of a milk carton. She goes through your drawers. She plays with the toothpicks, needling at her gums until they bleed. You want to tell her about your life; about your mother and father, about your strange half-moon birthmark, about the way your daughter hugs you, about the time you ran for social secretary in grade five and lost – but she anticipates you. She raises her hand to silence you, a toothpick poking out from her two front teeth. She says: Please. Let's just be really quiet today. As if, as if you haven't been quiet forever.

◉◉◉

Your daughter is working on a family tree. It is the kind of grade-two project that is supposed to encourage growth and understanding. You picture your daughter's teacher, pale like a lamb, with a crooked nose, eating broccoli salad and leafing through old family pictures. You can see how she has been overwhelmed by her own original idea. She is hopeful that her students will remember her fondly when they begin to car pool or divorce. You imagine your daughter's teacher taking bubble baths, perfuming the water with exotic pharmacy oils, and having occasional sex with a drama student who lives in her building. You don't mean to think these things, but really, you have enough homework as it is. Who does the teacher think does most of this work anyway?

It is time to cut things out of the garden. It is the season. If you keep moving things around, transplanting them from one place to another, maybe that is the secret, maybe that way you can keep everything alive. The point seems to be to keep moving around. It just depends what you mean by alive. Nothing really dies, it just changes shape. When your husband turns away from you in bed, he tells you not to worry, he tells you he is only facing you in a different direction. You cut the cabbage plant and use it as a centrepiece. You cut zinnias and dahlias. You cut chrysanthemums. Thick, boisterous mums that come inside and drop their petals everywhere. Every day you vacuum up the petals. You know you should make a potpourri, but you are weary and the dried petals remind you of ashes. Your daughter picks the leaves off flowers. She says she wants them for her family tree. But first she has to clarify. How many fathers? How many grandfathers? How many grandmothers? How many mothers?

You never realized how poisonous nature is. You only knew ivy and oak, and that was bearable, natural, avoidable. Your husband marches through the garden announcing danger like a general preparing. Don't eat the bulbs of the daffodils or the tulips, the narcissus or the lilies of the valley. Beware the seeds of the lupines. Even the delphinium can kill you. You can smell the changes in the air, a thin film of coolness trapped inside the end of summer. Soon the maple will not be able to support the leaves. It will need all its water and will have to let them go. You stand in the splendour of your catastrophic garden and explain to your daughter that really you only had one mother. The other was something you were split from. Dig up the cabbage plant to illustrate. Carry the plant into the house, trailing the earth behind you. Tell her how you grew somewhere else, separately, an entirely different personality. Show her how you grew. Repot and look proud. Not everyone can repot with such ease. Look, you say to your daughter. Same plant, different character. And, really, it does seem different to you, sitting there on top of your wooden table, a sort of strange collage of a tree.

Moments go by and you do not think of her. It is Halloween and your hands smell cold and earthy, like pumpkin. You eat roasted pumpkin seeds with your husband and watch a marathon of documentaries about octopuses. Your daughter is counting candy on the carpet at your feet. Every now and then she calls out like a fisherman declaring his catch: I got two black Twizzlers and three Whatchamacallits. She is huddled around her loot like the neighbourhood harpy in a befuddled costume that you had helped her make, and as you look at her now, dishevelled and gorging, you realize you have no idea what she is supposed to be. You tried your best to make her an atom, a thing you are just beginning to believe in (as though science, for the novice, is just another act of faith), something swirling and so essential. She tried to make herself a zebra, a wild thing with stripes, something real and recognizable. You know that your interpretation of an atom is all wrong; you have not given her orbitals or electrons, instead you have given her gauze and mosquito netting and silver chiffon scarves. Atoms — by Isadora Duncan. It is no longer chemistry. It is ballet, and you understand atoms as something wispy and evasive like spies or ghosts. She painted her face in lines of black and white and taped pointy triangle ears to her headband. Before she left the house, patient, good-natured, holding a mess of scarves in one hand and a plastic pumpkin in the other, she turned to you and asked: Mommy, what am I again? And you reassured her that she was special indeed, the most elemental zebra of them all, the beginning and the end of all zebras. Your husband raises his eyebrows. He is playful enough, but he does not approve of the lies the unscientific tell themselves. They are halfway down your walk, your daughter and your husband, holding hands, released into the night where the moon is full and the air smells like loss and burning leaves and you are still shouting after them: It is possible to be the *thing* and the *spirit* of the thing all at the same time. You close the door against the disguised night and you are thinking – if for no other reason than the fact that you have always been haunted, that in a world where people die and leave you, where you are always saying goodbye, and everyone in the end is essentially all right, is essentially resilient – this might as well be true.

The television says: When under stress, as in captivity, some octopuses will even eat their own arms, which grow back.

Your daughter is tired of sorting her treasure. Her face is smeared and runny, her black curls tinted accidentally white, and she looks strangely aged and haggard from begging for treats. She turns to you, sleepy and generous, and drops a handful of the dullest toffees in your lap. Here, she says. I hate these. You can have them all. She kisses you good night and her lips are sticky with lipstick and licorice, and you watch her drag her black mop tail wearily to bed. You and your man will spend the night chewing through the rejects of her pillage, picking thick masses of caramel from your teeth. You will try to talk but find that you cannot keep your fingers out of your mouth. It reminds you of so many Halloweens, of so many costumes: Little Red Riding Hood, the cat, the football player, the sexier cat, the even sexier cat, the enormous overgrown baby with a huge diaper and a jumbo lollipop. . . . So many costume changes, and your mother like a stagehand or prompter, raising the curtain, pushing you out, sewing up frayed hems, offering you her eyelashes or a girdle, anything for the sake of make-believe. These are things that you remember only after the candle has gone out in the face of the pumpkin. On the television you see the threatened octopus squirt a cloud of black ink into the water. And someone says: Some say the cloud takes on the shape of an octopus, leaving a phantom drifting in the water to confuse the predator while the real octopus makes a getaway.

Your father calls and says: Did you know how much a roast costs? Or a bell pepper? Or those Coffee Crisp things? Sometimes I imagine she's just in the bathroom. I followed her handwriting and made a soup.

You do a functions assignment and get an A. Your daughter gets a gold star on her family tree. She is very clever. She calls it her Ances Tree. You put both of them up, side by side on the fridge. Your husband, the one who smells like grooming powder, puts his arms around you both and calls you his smart girls. This is your daughter's family tree: a single twig in the centre of a piece of blue construction paper. Spreading out from the twig she has pasted cut-out leaves. In the centre of the leaves are tiny headshots of your family that your daughter has severed from their photographs. It should upset you; instead you think that it is right that somewhere in your photo albums there is real evidence that there are holes in your life, blank, empty circles where things are no longer complete. On the leaves, in clear block handwriting, it says: *This is my grandpa. I love him because he lets me shave his whiskers. This is my father. I love him because he is an animal man.* You have the grandest leaf of all. It is a terrible picture of you. You recognize it as the one from the beach. Your hair is tangled with salt water and you are picking sand from your eye. You are mouthing "no" at the camera. You follow the steady thickness of your daughter's letters. They say: *This is my mother. I love her because she has a split personality.* Beside this the teacher has pencilled in a frightened red question mark.

Two things happen at the clinic. Mrs. Ziggels' Shih Tzu drops dead while the groomer is tying a green ribbon in the dog's hair, and a thick white malamute goes into cardiac arrest during surgery. Your husband slices open the thorax and massages the heart in his hand, coaxing it to pump. He opens his arms to Mrs. Ziggels and holds her while she shakes. He spends the night lying beside the malamute. He kneels in puddles of urine and eases the animal towards morning with Valium and morphine. He watches for signs of brain damage and traces the word *miracle* with his finger, over and over again on his knee. You bring him chicken in the basket, and a variety pack of dry cereals. You play a couple of hands of crazy eights and then leave him to his healing. When you tell your daughter about the dogs, she starts to cry. She doesn't understand yet that a heart just suddenly gets exhausted and has to lie down. And neither do you. You tell her that there are many ways to die. Last year in your country two people died of rabies and one hundred people died when they shook a vending machine for that dangling chocolate bar and the machine came down on top of them.

You are making a map of your garden, trying to diagram which seeds were planted where and where they will appear in spring. You have so many things buried in your garden, it is always a surprise. The ground is frozen, neighbours still have their Christmas trees up, but you are beginning to be able to plan and foresee and it makes you feel real again. You are the species with the concept of soon or later. You are the only species that can imagine the future. This is the reason to plant. You can imagine spring and a softer ground. You can imagine a day without mumbling to yourself. And a day when you don't hear that final struggle in her small chest when you close your eyes.

●●●

Still, when you are cramming for finals and poisoning your family with frozen vegetable pies and leftover cauliflower surprise, she sprawls across your carpet, smoking filterless cigarettes and listening to your scratchy Bob Dylan albums. She is lazy and tired all the time. She wears sunglasses in the house, little round ones tinted blue, and nibbles at the cauliflower. She writes terrible poems about loneliness and Satan and children born without limbs. She stares into your closet for a long time and asks if she can borrow the pine-green blouse with the Chinese collar. It is like having another daughter around. You realize suddenly that you are older than she is. You watch her grow young, which is odd and impossible. You spend your days with your hands on your hips, saying: What are you doing? Stop that. She turns to you hopelessly one day, clutching a baggy red sweater to her chest. You won't let her borrow it. She is the kind of girl who takes but does not give back – who gives but does not take back. Help me, she says – slow, like she's pulling the words from another world. I'm pregnant. It has gone too far, this nonsensical haunting; still, you give her things.

Take the red sweater, you say. You give her the Dylan albums and a Baggie of carrots, dried prunes, and a small tangerine, for vitamins A, B, and C. You take her out to the garden and show her where you plan on growing the dicentras. You do not tell her that those are bleeding hearts, beautiful upside-down flowers dizzy with sadness, and when she turns to ask, you bolt inside the house and slam the door. She stands in your frozen garden, contemplating the cold earth, the icy rock garden, a very sad ghost. You lean against the door. You breathe. You let go. You ignore the mournful rapping while you do your twenty-minute workout.

●●●

First, we are not taught to grieve. And second, there is this urge to forgive. It is why we say: I'm sorry. You suddenly have the power to forgive great injustices, crimes and letdowns. This is the holiness of sorrow. It is almost nine months, and you are pushing the thing from you like a birth. The sky, though grey and heavy with snow, seems kinder. The bare trees, naked and skinny, seem vulnerable. There is a stone now, a marker forever – longer than her life. You stand there, your head wrapped in a scarf, stamping your feet at the edge of her grave – forgiving the world.

Your father calls and says: I tried Thai food. I sewed a button. There was an hour when I didn't think of her. Do you think that's all right?

Sometimes when you are grating carrots or pitting cherries and you are staring out your window, you think you see her standing on your corner, in a gold-and-brown skirt, shifting from hip to hip, just waiting. Sometimes you think you see her sunbathing on your front lawn. She waves at you, tries to get your attention, but you are reaching for the morning newspaper and you don't look up. Sometimes you see her kneeling in your garden, weeding, trying to be someone else. Most of the time you realize who you are missing and you bake something, a pie, a crumble, something that will overpower the house. You pass your exams. Someday you might even save a life.

THE THIRD PERSON

Here is an introduction. The fact is that sometimes it is very hard to get into a story, sometimes there is no smooth path to lead up to what has to be said. The road just ends, you have to hike for a while, and when you get there it's just a shack of a tale, with no running water. A good way to start is to say that there are many ways to hope and to leave. And there are many ways to be left. For instance, Elle's kind adoptive mother said to her: Here in the dictionary you can see that it says that left is towards the north when one faces east. This was the kind of thing Elle's adoptive mother would say. She was an avid crossword doer, and she used the dictionary fanatically for everything, like a sacred text. Later, after she died, Elle built herself a small wooden bookshelf and lined up her mother's dictionaries alphabetically. Oxford before Webster, Funk after College. *Look, there's no easy way to tell you this,* said Elle's mother, who believed in bluntness the way some people believe in love. *When you were born you were abandoned in an alley. When they found you, you were very cold and almost dead. And then you came to live with us.* Elle blinked. *I was found in a dumpster?* she asked, adolescent, lanky, incredulous. *Not in a dumpster. Beside one,* said her mother gently, as though it was the preposition of the story that was important. Later on, Elle found small clippings from a newspaper out west where they referred to Elle as poor and blue. Elle's mother believed in the lightning of emotions, the sudden flashy discharge of spark that could really only strike you once. *It's a good thing,* she said to her daughter. *That was your big hurt. Now nothing can touch you again.* And it was true that much later when her mother died, at first it was just like a rumbling with long pauses in between, spaces where you could count five, ten seconds, like a storm far, far away.

●━●

People are chaining themselves to things. It's a question of belief. They all look like prisoners in a gang of faith. Elle watches the demonstration on the news. The people carry signs that read ADOPTION IS THE LOVING OPTION. And BABY KILLERS GO TO HELL. Some of them are wailing in a spiritual agony. Others just look angry and tired. Elle envies their unwavering zealousness, their vitality, their energy. Where do they get so much energy? They seem to have a real flair for faith, as though it were a kind of style, a tricky thing to do with an accessory that only certain types could pull off. They light beautiful candles and hold a small child up above their heads to heaven, like a rowdy team. It is their certainty that fills Elle with longing, the way they assemble in packs and flaunt their loyalty. God must love them the way some people, not Elle, but people like, let's say, Elle's man, love their dogs. The night of the worst demonstration, where two doctors are shot and many are wounded in a terrible fire, Elle's baby is born.

●━●━●

The first time Elle sees her newborn daughter, she breaks out into a pocky rash and spikes a high fever that makes her shiver and giggle at the same time. Later, while she is resting, her hand travelling up and down the cream-puffiness of her belly, a nurse reveals to Elle that she had cried out in a kooky delirium: *Hallelujah. Hail the daughter. Hail the newborn queen.* Hail, thinks Elle. And then to her husband: Have I ever said the word 'hail' before? Elle's man holds the baby and shakes his head and she is surprised to see the redness of his eyes, and the way he swallows and swallows, the only way she has ever seen men cry.

The baby is astonishing. Everyone says so. Bored and surly nurses and perky lactation experts who have certainly seen too many engorged, hammy breasts take their time around Elle, stroking the baby and leaving the room, well, *stoned*, is the only way Elle can put it. High as a giraffe's eye, she said to her man, the veterinarian, who loves when she expresses herself in terms of animals. What Elle doesn't tell anyone is that sometimes while she is nursing the child, the smooth little infant mouth tugging at her nipple as though it was a kind of tough, goopy taffy, Elle can hear voices singing somewhere, a choir of sexless singers rejoicing, really, for what other word is there for that kind of noise, and to Elle's tired ears the words sound something very like: *Hail to the mother.*

·—·—·

Elle's husband is a veterinarian. His hospital is bright and cheery and smells like washed dogs. It is a smell that always makes Elle think of romance, with its black bags of needles and its medicine and intravenous lines, and the first time she kissed her vet in front of the cage of a dying hound dog. Or maybe it's just the groomed smell of devotion, the way the animals slam their tails against the sides of the metal cages, waiting, hoping, for surely someone will come for them. The first time they met, Elle had brought in a stray cat that she had seen hit by a car. She carried it in wrapped in her old green sweatshirt, and when it died she simply shrugged her shoulders and rewrapped her ponytail, which had come undone. You don't have to apologize to me, said Elle, when the vet lifted his sorrowful eyes to her, prepared for the worst. I've already had my big hurt. It was late in the night and he admired her for paying the emergency fee even though she hadn't known the cat. They sat together on the cement step outside the clinic and he shared some lukewarm tea with her from a broken Thermos. While they talked they watched a pigeon making its way slowly along the sidewalk, its beak hanging open in an agonizing pant. It turned up the walkway towards Elle, slumped to its side, and died at the tip of her shoe. Elle turned to her veterinarian, her face purposefully blank, and whispered: You have no idea. The weirdest things happen to me.

●━●

On the wall in the reception area of the clinic is a painted mural of Noah and his ark. In the centre of the ark is a crazy cartoon likeness of the veterinarian with his arms open and his mouth round and wide as though he was in the middle of an opera. The animals walk two by two away from the vet and though it is supposed to look as though they are disembarking onto safe dry land, the artist has forgotten to paint in the shore, so instead it appears that they are all being forced to walk the plank. I can't leave it like that, Elle has heard the vet say many times, but so far he has. It's true that there are a lot of similarities between Noah and the vet. For instance, he has two of everything. Two dogs, two cats, two fairly old goldfish, and two coral snakes. And, thinks Elle not quite unhappily, two women. Elle doesn't really mind. She believes whole-heartedly in alternates, understudies, runners up. She has never expected anyone's undivided attention. It is only after the baby is born that something begins to happen to her tone of voice, a flabbiness in the muscles and layers of her language that makes the vet suspect, if only slightly, a problem. A little while after the baby is born Elle says to her vet: I tried calling you all day but your assistant wouldn't let me through – is she new? Who? Bruno? the vet says, reaching up and pressing his thumb into his eyeball so that he can only see her out of one good eye, the way he always does when he is about to tell half a story. Elle asks: Your secretary's name is Bruno? It's just a nickname, the vet explains. He tries to make his voice neutral and bored, the familiar tone of office love, but instead his words are balancing towards her like adolescent gymnasts on the beam. Did I mention her father was a famous boxer from Latvia? And Elle can see suddenly that he doesn't believe she will really trouble him about all this. She sees his whole attitude dismount, a sprightly, successful routine.

Soon after, Bruno sends a little wooden angel head to hang on the wall, and a card that reads: I am very happy at you. God, says Elle. I don't think I've ever been attacked by happiness before. Bruno? What kind of name is Bruno? The vet reads the note and unwisely defends his assistant. It's funny, he says. She thinks your name is weird too. She asked me, 'What kind of name is Elle? In French it's just the third person.' Elle hangs the little wood angel up anyway. It hangs above the doorway like a hunting trophy.

●━●━●

The baby is born with two curled toes on her left foot. In a way, Elle feels relief at this tiny abnormality. It makes her feel she could never lose the baby in the hospital, or anywhere else for that matter. She will always know her by her foot. This knowledge makes Elle feel like a prince. It is a small thing, just one little thing, but still it stakes out its claim and settles in her like a pioneer. It is a sign. A mark. Of what, she isn't sure yet. Usually in cases like these, says the doctor, one of the parents has the same thing. Elle and the vet slip off their shoes and wriggle their ordinary toes at the doctor. Well, he says. Maybe in one of your families. Elle holds the baby's small foot and it disappears inside her palm. Look here, the way the fourth toe curls on its side like a comma or a cat resting, and the other, the baby toe, how it lies across the others like a small bridge.

For the first few weeks after the birth of the baby, Elle lies in the middle of her bed, staring up at the ceiling fan, watching the whirl of the blades spinning so fast she can't make out their shapes. She blinks hard to slow them down to a staccato beat, like a strobe light: pale, long bodies in a disco. This blinking seems to Elle like a way of seeing beyond, capturing the motion of life in tiny increments. Beside her, the baby sleeps, sometimes peacefully, and sometimes in fits and twitches, her tiny mouth puckered and suckling, even in her dreams, even when there is nothing there. Elle loves these kissy faces, this naive, infant flirting; still, every time she looks at her daughter she wants to cry. Slow, salty tears pool out the sides of her eyes, burning hot grooves across her face, hooping behind her ears like glasses. *Oh, woman,* Elle says, to the torn and swollen girl who might have dropped her in an alley some time long ago. *Oh, woman. I know what it feels like to want to push everything from you. But how could you?*

Why do they say actions speak louder than words? Who thinks things like this? What exactly does volume have to do with anything? Actions are mime, theatrics, you need a person there for the hand-to-hand combat of actions. But words, words are sneaky, like smells. Words are the snipers hidden in the upper windows. All of a sudden your still, quiet head is a perfect red target and you never see it coming. Elle cannot sit still when she thinks about the word *innocence.* Had she ever believed in the innocence of anything, of anyone? Had she ever before believed it was a real word, with real meaning? So she is surprised, flustered, to find that this is the exact word that comes to her when she looks at her baby, though she can't quite use that word exactly and so she chooses instead *blameless*, for what it isn't and not for what it is. Because, before all this, hadn't she always imagined that there was actually something slightly guilty about babies, the way they twist and flail like criminals, always resisting something, always bullying past the limits? But she was wrong. All her life she had been so wrong.

It's like this, Elle tells her man, when she can speak again, between episodes of crying and nursing, and all the other dehydrating mysteries of those early days. I feel motherhood coming at me like a subterranean mumbling. Small animals stop and spin their ears like satellites, and then get the hell out of the way. What she feels in her baby's presence is terrible unworthiness; her whole life, each and every graceless action, follows her in a jangling harem of inadequacies. Sometimes her breasts begin to leak, darkly seeping through her shirt like something possibly frightening: wounds, holes, cracks along the ceiling. Look at me, Elle blurts in a panic. I look like one of those bleeding religious statues. And then she rolls her eyes back into her head dramatically and sings *ahhh* in a long, high voice, a scary imitation of ecstasy. Look at me, she says again, her eyes, her mouth, her whole face hanging off itself, like a thing hit by a twister. Have I been blown apart or what? In her worst moments Elle knows she is not smart enough for any of this. And she is very afraid. She keeps hearing this singing, choral and moody, not anything she would have in her own head. To the sleeping baby beside her she says: Is that you? Is it?

She overhears her man say to his assistant, Bruno: I think she is suffering a depression. She likes the way he says it. It makes her feel like something natural, in a way, like a mountain with a blemish, or something living up at a different altitude from everything else. It isn't that, thinks Elle to herself. She holds the baby close to her face and breathes her in. She cannot stop smelling her. She looks at herself in the mirror and watches herself sniffing the baby's head. She holds the baby's cheek up to her own and it is as though their faces are hinged. She says to the new, confused family in the reflection: I live in the body of this child. I don't know exactly what I mean by this, but I am lost in the form of this baby.

⌖⌖⌖

The night Elle told the vet that she was pregnant, they went to a party at a friend's studio. He was a carpenter and built odd and unusable furniture out of beautiful wood. The music was painfully loud and people danced and clomped and sent sawdust twirling through the air like glitter. Elle stood in the corner biting splinters out of her fingers. She tried to find a place to sit but the furniture was arty and impossible. She found a huge rocking chair covered in nails, and a small, delicately carved chair with no seat. She made her way over to her man, who had found a pile of wood shavings to lie in. In the dim light he looked to her like a giant hamster and it frightened her the way she could actually see his tiny, quick heart beating underneath his fuzzy skin. It made her feel powerful, like a lab technician. It made her feel like experimenting. When she bent down to touch him, to scratch his belly, to calm him down, he said to her: I'm sure you've heard that sometimes we eat our young for no good reason at all.

Later that night, he put down the article he was reading, with its mean little title – "Infertility of the Bitch and Breeding Disorders" – and said to Elle: What I like best about you is that you are hard and flat. I like that you don't feed my dogs when they beg you, or talk to them in a high, mousy voice. I like that you don't linger sentimentally on any one part of my body. Yes, said Elle. I know what you mean. And it was true. She knew exactly what he was getting at, and saw that he was very afraid. How could anything be growing inside her? It seemed so impossible. It was true that she had always used attitude as a birth control and it had always worked; a narrow, squinted eye, an unyielding body that could fake any position, a soul so unromantic that for a long time she had never even had a telephone. She saw herself as a great relief to the vet, whose days were filled with people crumpling to the floor of his exam room in tears, and sad, uncomprehending animals who ended their lives folded over in a garbage bag and stuffed inside a tiny freezer. She knew that he especially liked the way she could imagine his life without her, the way she would fantasize a perfect woman for him, someone who flew a bush plane and photographed rare flightless birds of the Amazon. There's one for you, she might say, if they were walking down the street together, or running his dogs up over the mountain. And usually he'd agree. There would be something in the length of the hair or in the faded material of a jacket that would seem just right. I can't think of a single reason to bring a baby into our lives, said the vet, who had always been strict, some said even fanatical, about his spay and neuter policies. It's true, thought Elle, closing her eyes. There is nothing reasonable about it. It's just the stupidity of words, words like *baby* and *our life*, and all their terrible and imprecise definitions. There is nothing logical about the biological. Nothing, nothing at all.

Elle tried to have an abortion. She made the appointment and on that morning she and her man drove down the highway in the dawn of winter darkness, but when they got to the women's clinic, though it seems as impossible now as it did then, some

fanatical group had blown it up the night before. Elle and the
vet sat in the car and stared at the rubble and the police tape
that said DO NOT CROSS, and maybe it was the word *cross*, or
the way a crowd had begun to gather around the heap of the
fallen and abandoned building, chattering nervously, but Elle's
whole body was overcome by a hush, a deep, riveting silence
of religious proportions. Although it was still early in the
morning, they found a grimy all-night restaurant and had two
beers each, soft-boiled eggs in small tin egg cups, coffee, and
pulpy juice. Then the vet read the comics, the horoscopes and
the "Ask Your Veterinarian" while Elle threw up in the bathroom. Elle leaned up against the dirty sink, little dark flecks
of something – wet skin? – pooled around the edges of the
faucets. She ran her hands under the taps and looked at them,
her knuckles like rough miniature knees, the little half-moons
of her nails like setting suns, and she thought about how
everything really just looked like something else, you could go
on and on with the *like* of things, but eventually you'd have to
admit that things were just as they were. For here were her
hands. These were not the hands of a mother, their rough
selfishness, the way they took whatever they wanted with their
pinching fingers; and yet soon, here her hands would be, the
hands of a mother. On the drive home she stared out the
window at the flat redundant whiteness and wondered what
the baby would look like.

They decided telepathically. At first Elle imagined that maybe they were actually fighting, silently, wilfully, one stunned mind against the other. But soon he was passing her saltines and frozen-juice ice cubes, and rubbing her shoulders as she bent over the sink. Still, there were times when she would find him seated at the kitchen table, the paper spread before him and the picture of the bombed-out clinic. In one of the smaller local newspapers it was possible to make out, if they looked really carefully, the front end of their parked car. Elle would watch his big head begin to shake back and forth, and then this odd smile would edge its way across his lips, the fleshy ledges of his face, a daredevil smile that made Elle slightly jumpy, that made her wonder what he saw when he looked at her. Incredible things happen to you, don't they? he said. There's just something about you that is beyond belief. Like there's belief, he said, slamming his hand down on one side of the table. And there's you, he said – slamming his palm down at the other end, his arms as wide as they could reach – somewhere at the far end and behind. Waving your arms. Jumping up and down.

For weeks, maybe even months, Elle sipped ginger tea and ate toast crusts all day long in front of the television. Once, she saw a talk show where a young fool of a girl tried to have an abortion. She visited some quacky doctor in a dirty corner of some American city and he didn't seem to notice that she was already eight months pregnant before he performed some carving procedure and a few days later this moronic girl went into labour and her baby was born with only one arm. The other arm was just all raggedy at the shoulder where it had been severed. The girl sat there with her long, shaggy black hair practically covering her eyes. Her baby, with the same shocky splash of black hair, slept peacefully, wrapped in a white swaddling blanket that looked to Elle like a huge wrap of gauze, as though the little baby were just one big wound. The girl talked about the awful instruments the doctor had used, and then she told the audience that her baby was an instrument of God, as though God was really just a spiffed-up bandleader, and Elle tried to imagine this gentle angel baby playing any one instrument with her one strong arm, her one good hand, like maybe one bongo, or half a guitar. And then she remembered something about an old jazz piano player who had had a stroke and kept on playing with just one good hand, and Elle thought that maybe everything could be okay for this little girl, just maybe. Believe me, she said to the television. It's good to get your big, jagged hurt out of the way. At night, both Elle and the vet shared the same dream where the baby was born with the bomb switch clutched in its bully fist.

All Elle wants to do now is sing a proper lullaby, something about bunting and hunting or falling out of a tree, but each time she holds the baby in her arms, all she can come up with are hits from the seventies and Christmas songs. She doesn't know which of these frightens her more. She hums the "Hustle" and then breaks into something by the Electric Light Orchestra, but very soon she finds herself rocking to "O Come All Ye Faithful," and more times than she can count the baby has fallen dreamily to sleep with "Silent Night." It's the word *holy*, she thinks. And *hark*, and *triumphant*. Okay already, she hears her man hissing through the closed door. Enough with the carolling. When he holds the baby he only sings Dylan, though once when he was fumbling around he launched into the Meow Mix song followed very quickly by the theme for the Oscar Meyer Wiener. But that was only once. Sometimes Elle imagines that he will take the baby away from her and raise her himself, and when he will speak of her to the daughter he will lower his voice to a scratchy whisper as though he were telling a ghost story.

●━●

It is a biblical summer. People are wearing tunic dresses, short and long, and everyone is wearing these open-toe sandals. Elle's man clomps across the floor like Moses. Elle sighs when she sees his toes. The punched-out swollen bulbs of the big ones, and the head-shrunken nuggets of the little. Feet, and all their webbed innuendoes, have always made Elle nervous. It seems to Elle, while she sits on her stoop with the baby pressed against her chest, that the whole world is slapping by in breezy flip-flops. Some are good for hiking big mountains. Others have little leather sheaths that hold the big toe like a bullet. Elle watches her neighbours suspiciously, their toes naked and splayed, and she imagines that they are all followers of some cult. She herself wears closed sneakers and the baby wears tiny socks with thin rubber grips at the bottom. They sit on the stoop, their feet all obscure, like heretics.

Elle goes to pick her baby up and finds her in her straw day-basket, pushing down on her palms, her little head straining to keep itself up. She looks at Elle, surprised as though she'd been caught exercising. Hey, you, Elle says, leaning down into the basket. You're too young for that kind of aerobics. Elle picks her up and holds her high over her head and she feels suddenly a warm breeze swirl around the room. Elle thinks she hears a harp and decides it must be the wind chimes on an outdoor tree. The baby gives her her first smile, a sly dimpling in her cheeks that Elle mistakes for gas. And then she hears something, a hint of a sound, a bare suggestion of a whisper that sounds like: *Don't be afraid. I am with you.* Yes, says

Elle to the slamming in her chest, the shy galloping of her heart. And then: But how do I know that's a good thing?

◒◒◒

The first time Elle slept with her vet she tried to think of something sexy and reassuring to say and instead told him the odd and improbable facts behind her birth. He held her and felt her inky boldness rubbing off on him like a huge tabloid headline. He kissed her softly on the forehead. His dogs, two fat Labs, stood around the bed like columns, or voyeurs, or scientists, thought Elle as she closed her eyes, listening to the panting. Afterwards they held each other and waited, waited for the frightening words that might come out of someone's mouth after loving. Why don't you try to find your mother? the vet asked, and Elle replied cold and serious: I don't know. Why don't you buy yourself a mobile home? And forever after, it was like a routine between them: whenever the vet thought he saw a heavy silence bundling Elle, wrapping her up in an impenetrable stoniness, he would inquire, as though it were something curable: Why don't you try to find your mother? Stop saying that, Elle would say. Stop saying that as though it's a gynecological problem.

The second time they traded fantasies and ate some kind of slushy Chinese food in bed. He told her slowly how he wanted to do it under the moon on the ruins of Tikal, and she told him how she wanted to be hit on the head so hard that she got amnesia. Why? asked the vet, calling the dogs up onto the bed, for warmth, for protection. I don't know, said Elle. I look at my life and I don't really want to be there in person. I'd rather hear it all from someone else. I'd rather be there, say, in the third person. What I like best about you, said the vet, smoothing down her tangled hair, is how far away you are. It will take a lot to get to you.

He tried, a few times it seemed, to make her dream come true. He tried to bring on the shock of forgetfulness by whispering to her over and over again: *You don't know anything. You don't know anything.* Elle thinks that this is how the baby was conceived, in a flurry of forgetfulness while two strange people tried to build a memory. What a dumb and fickle thing a memory is, thinks Elle. Here's the question: Why won't the baby remember what it was like to live in my body and then in my arms. What is the significance of this amnesia? And why, thinks Elle, is it then possible for me to remember all the radio hits of the seventies?

When Elle was eighteen she received an impossible letter in the mail from her real mother. In one corner of the envelope was a stamp with a rodeo scene, and in the other was a return address. *Despite what you might think, I was relieved to know that you made it through that long, savage night. Please try and find a place where you can think of me without cringing. If I never hear from you I will understand.* Oh no you don't, thought Elle, folding the letter and hiding it in an old wooden recipe box. Her hair turned to static, and what she felt surging through her was just the briefest feeling of near miss.

●━●━●

Elle brings her baby to the doctor. There's something wrong with her, she tells the doctor. She hardly fusses. She's always warm. And when she touches you, there's always a little tingling where her body has been. If something's not the matter now, I'm pretty sure it will be soon. The doctor looks at Elle and smiles at her the way he smiles at all first-time mothers, with squinted eyes and flat closed lips. Elle looks at the doctor's shoes and sees that he wears loafers, finally shoes with closed toes. She doesn't think she could bear looking at anyone else's feet. Elle is about to say more about her baby, how one day she looked into the deep, dark centre of her flying-saucer eyes, and saw an orange flame dancing in her eyeball, thrusting and twisting like a modern dancer in bright spandex, and how she was mesmerized for hours as she watched and the baby seemed to sleep with her eyes wide open. . . . But the doctor puts his stethoscope in his ear and leans over the baby to listen to the whoosh and drumming of her blood. He stretches her out and measures her all around, noting the numbers in his file with the precision of a tailor. He tells Elle that her baby is fine. Right as rain, is what he says. He picks the baby up and presses her against his chest. Elle can see how his eyes droop just a little and his shoulders fall slightly the way they do when someone is touched unexpectedly in their weakest and favourite spot. Elle waits. Umm, the doctor says, handing the baby back finally. I feel excellent today, he says. Don't you? Elle nods and backs out the door. She can hear other children crying in the waiting room. She wills herself not to look at the doctor but she can't help it, and there it is, that weird pinkish glow, as though the sun had just set around him.

●●●

At five and a half months the baby begins to crawl and Elle bursts into tears. Don't push yourself so hard, she weeps, seizing up the baby and smothering her against her chest. Just try to be a little more average. People in the neighbourhood

stop her on the street and say in voices that Elle finds frightening: She's crawling? Really? And then they look at Elle, her
plain, serious face, her ordinary posture, and the anxious way
she squints at everyone, nodding her small head like a finch,
and she knows that they are trying to imagine how anything
so supernatural could be born to someone so ordinary. And
when the baby starts walking unnaturally early, Elle scoops
her up whenever she notices someone staring, and pins her
hard against her body.

Elle has always been afraid of children and now she knows
why. They mingle outside her house and ask to hold the baby.
They all have pet rats, Elle has never seen so many rats, and
she wonders about the plague. One girl with long, skinny legs
is cross-eyed and pigeon-toed and when she holds the baby
her whole body straightens and aligns itself, as though she's
suddenly been aimed in the right direction. Another names
her shiny plastic doll after the baby, which scares Elle because
it makes her think of voodoo. Others are just too smart and
so mean. One of them, the one with the rat perched on her
shoulder like a miniature wrap, looks at Elle and says: My
mother says you can tell already that your baby will be
nothing like you. And then another looks at Elle's jeans with
the shabby holes and adds: Is there a reason why you always
wear the same ugly pants? I'm so afraid of her, she tells her
veterinarian, I mean for her. I meant to say I'm so afraid *for*

her. Word gets around. From her window Elle can see people standing at the edge of her lawn, waiting.

Elle watches the television while the baby plays with the colour knob, the contrast, the volume. Sometimes the baby does such baby things – marching around the house with her tiny sneakers in her hand, yelling suddenly at the top of her lungs, calling after the cat, drawing out the *a* of the word, making it the longest word she knows – *caaaat? caaaat?* – gripping Elle's knees and trying to hoist herself up like a mountain climber, and then falling defeated in a heap to the floor – that for a moment Elle imagines that maybe she is wrong. On the television a safety expert is teaching children to be street-smart. Remember, he says. A stranger can look just exactly like you. When the vet gets home he asks Elle: What's with all the people outside? Elle is on the floor building a tower of blocks with the baby. Oh, says Elle slowly. The baby healed that cross-eyed girl. The vet does not know what to say. He is not used to his new family and all their oddball parlour tricks. So he says: Maybe it's time you found your mother.

While her family is sleeping, Elle calls the New Mind Alliance. For \$5.99 a minute maybe someone can answer all her questions. Elle loves the word *alliance*. The very triangleness of the word makes her happy. It reminds her of treaties and unions and space-world federations where everyone has a huge and lumpy forehead but is basically a good and righteous creature all the same. She tries to ignore the sound of *lie* in the word. She concentrates instead on the *ance* part of the word, like ants, those industrious, hard-working colonials. Or *ance* that rhymes with dance and romance. And underpants, she hears the voice of her veterinarian say, although he is sleeping in the next room. The line rings a few times and then a psychic operator picks up the telephone and says: Money, love, or work? Elle isn't prepared for this choice. Is that it? asks Elle. Aren't there any other choices? Her psychic doesn't answer and then Elle hears a click and realizes a minute has gone by. Look, says Elle quickly. What I want to know really is how I would know for sure if my baby was the Saviour? As in, the Anointed One, the Redeemer, the Daughter of God, blessed be She. The psychic says: You think your baby is the Saviour? Look, that just isn't in the realm of questions I can answer. Elle runs her fingertips over the push-button numbers of the telephone. She thinks of them as a message to her. The pound key. The star. The zero. If it helps any, says the psychic, I see that he loves you very much.

●━●

For a little while Elle worked at the clinic, cleaning cages and washing torn and soiled towels. She had a way with the fiercest cats, the ones who would lunge their nervy bodies against the cage doors, their hooked little nails scything the air, looking for the pale wheaty colour of Elle's skin. But she would stun them with her quick nonchalance, the way her arm didn't seem to care what they did to it. In a brief second, she would grab them by the neck and toss them into new cages. But this was still early in their relationship, Elle's and the vet's, when at night she might read to him from a little bundle of stories she had written all about birth mothers and daughters and their bad, failed attempts at reunion. In one story a mother and daughter suffer from a sort of degenerative eye disease and both go silently blind and apathetic before they find each other. In another, the daughter almost makes it to a nudist colony where she will see her mother for the first time, but impulsively she takes off her tank top while driving along a country road, and it gets stuck over her eyes and she careens off the shoulder of the road, flipping terribly into a ditch. I don't know, said the vet, quietly, carefully, the first time she read to him. It just seems to me that your people need to find each other. Otherwise, they'll all go mentally ill. He held his finger to his head, twirling it at the temple, and made the cuckoo face. He said: I have seen dogs, tormented and conflicted in their very nature. They spin circles, they snap at invisible flies, they bark at a spot on the wall forever.

●—●—●

Elle gets into bed beside her man and says: I think our baby is God. Her husband is distracted, reading a medical journal with a picture of a sliced-up bloated heart. It was this man who told her that it is scientifically possible to be born with your heart in the wrong place. Did you hear what I said, Elle asks, shifting onto her side, feeling the heavy tugging of her huge breasts, *heaving breasts*, thinks Elle, *I have heaving, gasping breasts*. She's pretty special, says her husband. She's pretty unbelievable. No, says Elle, with a staccato urgency that makes him lick his lips. She raises her eyes to the ceiling and says: I mean like God, really God, God-God. He switches off the light and in the dark Elle tells him about the strange light she's seen around the baby, about the choir of voices that she can't get out of her head, about the little singes of electrical heat that crackle through her every time she picks up the child. What have I done with my stupid little life? cries Elle. What will I do? I just don't think I'm actually the type to be the Mother of God. I've been bad. I've inhaled. I've tried my whole life to feel nothing. I've let you cheat on me. None of this is Virgin material. In the dark she can hear the vet holding his breath. She counts the seconds, waiting for the big exhalation, but it seems she falls asleep before it ever comes.

Elle holds the baby. She dances. She twists and shooby-doos across the floor imitating carefree, something she saw in a commercial once for soap. Or was it tampons? She prays for

her baby. *You will be regular. You will live a plain life with no surprises.*
Also, says Elle aloud this time. You won't be the kid in the
schoolyard who stands around the garbage can talking to the
insects. She doesn't actually think of this as praying. More
like calling in requests to a radio station she doesn't get. But
she knows that what she is hoping for is impossible, that there
is nothing ordinary about what she is dealing with. Easter
passes, stupid holiday of rabbits and chickens, and Elle says
odd and inconceivable things to the veterinarian whose office
is full of dying chicks and dehydrated bunnies. What is it
about the mothers of gods? asks Elle. Why can't they do more
to protect their children?

Elle's husband has taken to calling the baby the Big Cheese.
So, he says when he comes through the door, how's the Big
Cheese? Elle cringes a little when he says it but thinks that
at least it's better than what he'd been calling her before. He
would see the baby sitting up straight in her high chair, drinking perfectly out of her little cup, and he would announce:
Look everyone. It's the Queen of the Juice. It occurs to Elle
that the baby is tenderly indulgent with her father, leaning
her head against his shoulder, pulling at his ponytail, pointing to his feet when he asks her where they are, and Elle begins
to imagine that the baby has come to them because they are
both, in effect, blessed idiots, sacred simpletons. Sometimes
at night, when the vet is late at the hospital, wrestling the

animals with his Bruno, Elle falls asleep on the couch and has dreams that are bleak and frightening, like documentaries. Women vaporize with the sound of singed hair and babies crawl across their shadows looking for food, for laps, for bends in an arm, anything three-dimensional. Elle shaves her head. She leaves just a thin pile across her scalp like a swatch of gold velvet. Oh my God, says the veterinarian, looking at her long, bony body and her small, shocking head. You look like an exclamation point, those Spanish upside-down exclamation points. It's true, now, that there is something about her that seems abrupt. There is a new suddenness about her, as though she could begin or end or change any minute. Not an exclamation point, thinks Elle, but a small *i*, a tiny *i* that sees everything. The baby reaches up and touches her mother's new head, smooth as a moose, soft like young antlers. Her smile is still fleshy, little round pulpy buds instead of teeth. All the other babies on the street have teeth, two on the top, two on the bottom; Elle has to try hard not think of them as rodents. Elle worries that her baby will never learn to seize. When she smiles she looks gentle and raw, like the inside of the mouth of a fish.

The baby is telling Elle to do things. For instance, she is fastidious about washing out the recyclable cans and plastics before putting them in the green box. It's true, Elle told the vet. She's absolutely right. What good am I doing just passing on my muck and dregs to someone else? She scrubs cans and peels labels, even the horrible old jars of salsa that they would usually just let collect in the fridge because they couldn't bear to deal with them. Elle counts out fifteen old jars of salsa and cleans them all, the baby riding on her back in a baby-pack. Just that morning Elle was changing the baby's diaper, bending down to blow a cheerful raspberry on her smooth pokey belly, when she felt a tiny hand lifting her chin, and the eyes of her child piercing right through the sad, loose sack of her heart, and heard words, woolly and thick as blankets: *Even in your darkest hour, my child. . . .* Look, said the vet. If she was God she wouldn't break down crying every time you left the room. And she'd be toilet trained. And she'd part her bath waters. And she wouldn't suck her blanket.

●━●

Once, early on in their relationship, Elle asked him about his image of God. She was lying in his bed, the sheets pulled up to her neck to protect herself against the beefy-tongued dogs. Elle had been trying to imagine this as an aerial view, the raft-like way the whole brood clung to a bit of mattress, and just this idea of being looked down upon made her ask him. He told her emphatically that he didn't have an image, no not at all, but when she pushed him, he ended up describing a really big guy with bad teeth, like a hockey goalie, making saves, winning the game. Elle said: I wish I believed in something. Anything at all, really. I don't even believe in sports, the muscling pastime of it, the spirit of jesting. The vet kicked the dogs off the bed and Elle took it as a gesture of love. They moaned as their paws hit the floor, and then slunk under the bed. Elle fell asleep to the sound of their tails thumping, underneath her and thought of a big god with thick, puffy knee pads, a mask, and a big stick, and wondered why everything that was supposed to be good and restoring seemed essentially put there to scare her.

●━●━●

The baby tells Elle to prepare for certain eventualities. In case of an earthquake she packs a duffle bag full of old, warm clothes, blankets, and shoes, and leaves it on a heavy hook by the front door, ready to go. She renews their passports. She buys food in tins and fills boxes with what she likes to call her provisions. The baby waddles and lurches across the floor and drops a can of beans into a box. Elle prepares tiny kits in little plastic bags. A sewing kit with threads in every colour. A first-aid kit with Band-Aids, and ointments, and plastic gloves. And other bags of odds and ends. Jewellery she wore in high school, fat, hollow hearts and a sparkling poodle pin. The veterinarian's graduation pen. A black cigarette holder from an antique store. Some new floppy discs. The vet holds up the plastic bags and swings them back and forth in front of Elle's face. For barter, she says, and the veterinarian sighs. Look, he says. Obviously having a kid is bringing some stuff up. . . . Elle stops him with a wave of her hand and when she speaks she is surprised to find her voice so shrill, so almost out of tune. She rises up on her tiptoes and balances there like a dancer. This is how she finds herself walking around lately, up on the balls of her feet, her soles high above the floor. Look, she says. It's all very fine for you. You're a doctor. They'll always need doctors. Me and her, Elle points to the baby who has climbed up on one the boxes, we'll be the first ones marched to the camps. The veterinarian is exhausted. Sometimes it's easier when your patients can't tell you where it hurts, when the worst they can do is bite you. Camps? he asks. What camps? I don't know, whispers Elle. Ask her. She points to their daughter, who is walking away from them with her shoe in her hand, talking to herself like a delirious old person; a thin rim of something bright surrounding her small body, she hums like a neon light.

Later, Elle says to the vet: Look, I don't think I'm right about the camps thing. Sometimes it's so hard to hear what she is trying to tell me. All I know is that she keeps asking me if I'm ready.

The vet is frightened of the shape of Elle's breakdown, a kind of squiggly mess of undefined edges. He works late at the clinic with his assistant, often spending nights on a wretched cot, coming home and complaining about his back. When Elle imagines him and his assistant she thinks of odd euphemisms like *putting to sleep* and *passing the clamp*. He is very afraid of people going crazy. When he was in school he lived with a roommate named Max Eggles who went mad. Instead of studying for exams he sat cross-legged on the floor and watched game shows all day long because he liked to see people win. Later, the vet went to visit him in an institution, where Eggles sat all day in a bathrobe and brown knee-high socks, his mouth hanging open like a flap of a tent. The vet hid his horror, called his friend Scrambled Eggles behind his back, but Elle could see the seriousness in his face when he said the word *crazy*. This is what he says to Elle: I liked you better when you were cold and distant, like a northern place, uninhabited, hard to get to. Now you're like some tourist trap, crowded, tacky, too close to the highway.

●━●

Elle finds a lump on the baby's body, just below the sticky little crevice of her armpit. She is sitting in the tub with the baby, pouring little shampoo caps of water onto the baby's hands while the baby giggles. Just like a regular baby, thinks

Elle. She runs her hands along her daughter's body, feels the fruity lump, moves away to wash another part, a strong, smooth leg for instance, and then returns tentatively to the lump. Elle takes the bunny-shaped washcloth and presses it over her own terrified face, trying to stop the thumping in her eyes. She can sense the baby waiting, the little breath of a smile forming, thinking this is just another game of peek-a-boo. She waits for a long time and doesn't cry and though it seems like the water should be getting colder, it doesn't, and long after it's really possible, swirls of steam still rise up to the damp, mottled ceiling.

Just tests for now, says the doctor, trying hard to reassure Elle. But he cannot help himself; the truth, or some odd form of it, is pushed from his mouth: It's very rare, highly unusual, in all my career I have never . . . Elle notices a dotted cut along the doctor's hand when he goes to pick her baby up, like a thin string of scabby pearls, but when he hands her back, she sees that the cut is gone. Afterwards, Elle takes the baby to the park, a small, ugly city park with one rickety slide and a few rusty swings, and she pushes her back and forth in the baby swing and each time her hands touch the small perfect back of her child, each time she nudges her forward with the softest touch, she thinks: Please. Please explain to me what it means to be chosen. Soon, the baby reaches her arms up to Elle. Time to go, Elle hears her say, although she is sure her lips haven't moved. When Elle gets home she sees that people have begun congregating in flocks, some on the sidewalks, others on their own lawns. Is it the sudden cooling weather or is it something else? Some are in sandals, but most are barefoot now, pulling up clumps of grass with their big puffy toes, like sheep grazing. They are waving to Elle and Elle thinks she can hear them saying: Can't we just touch the baby? Just one little squeeze, a brush, the very tippy-tip of her hair, the soft bump of her crooked little toe?

Elle is standing in her dusty closet throwing piles of clothes to the floor, beside the baby who is helping her pack. She keeps waiting to hear the music that has been following her around, that vesperal humming that she has come to think of as the white noise of her brain, but all is strangely quiet. She stuffs a handful of diapers into the bottom of her bag and the baby pulls them out again. Hey, says Elle. Remember, this was your idea. All of Elle's clothes look too big for her and for a moment it seems as though she is in fact packing someone else's suitcase, a giant's perhaps. Elle knows she has lost too much weight. She is thin and fine like a clothesline and things just hang off her as though they were clipped there. She looks down at herself and her body seems to her unbearably stark and meagre, her knobby stork legs, her spiny, knotted back. Lookit, says Elle, grabbing back the diapers, her makeup case, a tube of diaper-rash ointment, all the things the baby has undone. I am still the mother here. And then suddenly the music is back, harps, harps, and more harps and she hears the baby say: *Shush now, I say unto you: You will find your way to me through this terrible storm.* Oh, speak English, will you, thinks Elle, roughly zipping her bag shut and lifting the baby up to the hard ridges of her chest.

●━●━●

On the bus Elle holds the baby against her and watches the slits of her sleeping eyes in the dark window. She hums in her sleep, high, delicate notes. Elle lies to a woman in a velvet skirt sitting next to her and says that this poor baby's mother died and she is delivering her to her grandmother. The woman clucks and shakes her head. The things you hear on buses. At the next bus station Elle calls the vet from a pay phone. Bruno answers and says that he is in the middle of a cat spay. Elle says: Let me talk to him. Tell him I'm going to find her. Elle hears the assistant mumble something to him and imagines her pulling the long, coiled cord into the surgery room and holding the phone up to the vet's masked face. What's all the racket, he asks, angry, unsure. It sounds like a goddamn bus station. When she tells him that it is a bus station his voice becomes an alarming rumble, the sound of furniture being moved along the dark floor of his mouth, the sound of moving out. Where's the baby, he asks. Here, says

Elle evenly. On the floor of the phone booth. Playing with cigarette butts and hypodermic needles, touching the palms of the homeless and destitute. Don't joke, says the vet. She could be very sick, you know. Come home. I'll stop seeing Bruno. Elle hangs up the phone and the rush of distance between them knocks Elle off guard for a moment, so that she has reach down and press her hand against the soft head of her child to stop her own shaggy, dizzy heart. *Come for me,* she whispers to him, in the small, stale time capsule of the telephone booth. *Come for me,* she says again and again, until she doesn't know what she is saying, maybe she is saying *comfort me.* Suddenly everything in the world seems retrievable but fleeting. You can find anything. Babies, mothers, feelings you never thought you had. All of it. Elle feels for the folded envelope in her back pocket, the envelope with the stamp of the rodeo, and she imagines hiring a private eye to help her, she imagines calling up some man in a soft, worn trench coat, but not being able to come up with anything to say, just a kind of personal, singular stuttering: *I . . . I . . . I . . .* , which would be a start anyway.

It's true that Elle's heart has always been a crab scuttling sideways. Turn her over like a rock or a sea shell and there's her little clawed heart digging into the sand. Some people approach everything on the diagonal, even the truth, and especially love. Poor love, thinks Elle. Poor overused love, so desperately in need of another word for itself. Elle feels her small guardian angel press up against her knee. Yes, I know this is something, thinks Elle. Love or whatever. The question is, she asks anyone, silently, Who wants to feel this bad? No one can make things right for another person, and yet, Elle wonders, slightly dazed and hypoglycemic from her effort to run away, is that my daughter, walking away in her flowered running shoes, with sure and unnatural steps, across the dirty, scraped floor of the bus station? And is that her, reaching out to that limp, sad woman slumped to her knees and leaning against the wall? And is that her, touching the quarter in the woman's muddy, etched hands and playing her fingers like a slot machine until the woman's hands are overflowing with shiny quarters spilling over into her lap and onto the floor? Is it only in Elle's imagination that all the buses are suddenly on time, and no one is looking quite so lost and the sandwiches in the cafeteria are no longer sopped with grease, and the waitresses are wiping their eyes and going home to people who really love them?

❧❧❧

Who can end a story like this, an impossible story where a baby is found in a rubbish heap and grows up to have a child who is a god? It isn't true that stranger things have happened. Stranger things have never happened. The thing about children, the absolute worst thing about children is that they are not at all like friends. Instead, thinks Elle, they are like awful acquaintances who pull you into their little karaoke clubs and force you to sing these hokey songs about hope. And that is what hope does to Elle. It makes her giddy and unreliable. It is like lip-synching. It can be so impressive, so tricky, if done right you could win contests. But mostly you just end up looking bonkers. Maybe that's the other thing about having children. Maybe the trick is for no mother to raise her own. Maybe that's just asking way too much of someone. So this is what Elle thinks as she waits for the bus heading west, imagining her own mother as a kind of cowboy, with a big hat and huge pointy boots that leave deep impressions in the ground. *When it gets really bad, I'll just pretend I'm her babysitter. I'll carry her around on my high, pointy hip, I'll introduce her to the shapes and colours of everything and I'll try to ignore all her little miracles. I'll tell her gently that she doesn't have to try so hard to be my baby. I'll tell her that I'll be right here. That I'll be right here until her mother gets back.*

CAN YOU WAVE BYE BYE, BABY?

It is surprisingly easy to run out of love. You do not chug or lurch suddenly like a car, coughing every few steps. You don't scream or bellow like the heaving hot-water taps. If someone shook you side to side like a milk carton, they wouldn't know that you were almost out, down to the last drop. There is no warning. It is so sudden, you cannot imagine there was ever any to begin with. Hardly anything else in the whole world disappears quite that easily, without a shudder. For the first two weeks when you held the baby in your arms you thought you felt something, something fishy maybe, the sensation you get when you hold a small guppy in your cupped hands and you can feel it twitching against the sides of your palms, quick little flutters, desperate. Now when you look at her face, her eyelids raw from crying, her fists curled under her chin as though in prayer, it is as though you have swallowed a cold, round river stone.

She is not feeding well. Your breasts are rocky and engorged. The best thing to do is to express yourself. You look down at her soft, unfinished head, and say: I don't think I will ever really love you.

The first time you do it, you are shivering so hard, tingling in all the creases of your skin, that after so long you can almost mistake it for a kind of horniness. The word *erotic* is in your head. Your heart is a heavy African drum, calling . . . calling. . . . The humid night air settles like pollen on your bare arms, empty now, light, dusted with baby powder like moth wings. Walking away from your house, you are surprised at how far you get, that there is nothing physically holding you back, no elastic band, or choke chain and leash. You look like anyone, walking. What did you imagine? Your dress lifts a little in the breeze. Everything conspires to tease you. At the corner store you think the word *cigarette*. It comes so quickly after the word *erotic* that you think that maybe you are becoming yourself again. The moon is a full, pink flush. Outside the store with the red awning, teenagers balance on their bicycles, one hand leaning against the brick wall. The girls break their popcicles in half against the sharp corner of the wall and demonstrate a blow job, their mouths, lips, and tongues staining dark purple. The group rides away laughing. A man stands with his dog. He is trying to light a match. The dog jumps up and the man curls his fingers into a neat fist and sends the dog hurling to the ground. *Hey,* you say, before you even realize that you are talking. The man turns to face you and his face seems damaged. His beard is uneven, his nose is flattened almost to his lip. Later, you will think that it is exactly how you pictured the face of an angel, challenging, ugly, filled with all the world's venomous wishes. *Then take him, bitch,* he says, throwing the leash at your feet. He turns away, running down the street, his thin, long black coat flapping like a crow. The dog doesn't move. He looks dazed and there is a bit of drool hanging from his black lips. You stand squinting after the shape of the man as though trying to read something on his back, trying to be a good witness, and think that, really, people should be made to wear licence plates. No matter what, you ought to be able to track them down. You thought you had dried up. But as you are walking home, the dog walking slowly behind you, you feel your milk pooling against the inside of your dress, trickling down between your ribs like sweat.

Newborns cry without tears. It is the only thing about them that is not liquid, and it surprises you. The point is that some things are just not yet fully formed and in a way you imagine that this is buying you some time. You lean over her crib and your face hovers just above hers like a blank moon. Her arms flail and her legs kick in short jerky movements. You cannot figure out if she is simply panicking or if she is trying to throw herself right at you, propel herself with such force out of her crib that you are forced to catch her. You have seen many diaper commercials. Women with neat hair pulled back in headbands, their hands pink and clean, their rooms flooded with sunshine. You imagine yourself saying: Who's wet? Who needs a changing? Are you mommy's best girl? Are you? But you do not like the sound of your voice, high and sexless like a cartoon character or someone going crazy, and all these one-sided conversations can't possibly prepare you for the arguments to come. You can tell already. She is wilful. She will fight you tooth and bone. Already your nipples are cracked and bruised and she is only using her gums.

•••

When they let you out of the hospital, all you could think was, *There must be some kind of mistake.* You stood there, leaning against the railing of the wheelchair ramp, watching the ambulance men drinking coffee straight from a Thermos. It seemed to you that you shouldn't be allowed to just walk out of a hospital with a baby in your arms without some sort of alarm going off, bells ringing, some warning that announces to one and all, the whole world, really, that here comes a mother. Watch out. Watch over her. In the maternity ward couples packed their bags together, fathers held their small bundles awkwardly, looking towards their women, who were already, in such a short time, experts. A nurse asked you if you would be all right, but before you could answer her, find out just what she meant, she became busy with a young couple who knew her by name, and they seemed to have a lot to laugh and reminisce about. The young mother was blushing. Surely they had all shared an intimate moment together. You do not recognize anyone. You look away from faces, or through them. As for this whole thing, you seem to only remember seeing the tops of your knees, first covered in a white sheet, and then exposed and red.

At the time, it struck you that this was the only occasion where you actually left the hospital with something in hand. Mostly, stuff is left behind. You felt conspicuous with your package wrapped and bound in white like a tiny crazy person being subdued. You wondered why there weren't more people like you, wandering around outside the hospital doors with their various parts, tumours, amputated legs and breasts, ovaries, excess fat, fibroids the size of eggplants. You sat at the bottom of the ramp, laughing out loud at the thought of people and all their parts flagging down taxis, going home. It is so obvious what you have done, what has happened to you. You remember looking around for others like you, but it seemed you were alone, the only one there on the ramp that morning. Somehow, real families must know something you don't. Somehow, real families must all leave through some other door. You saw a cop, a garbage can, a crying woman, an empty car, a tall bush, a white line down the centre of the road. All these different ways you could give up. It took a long time for your heart to stop beating so fast. In the taxi, out of habit, you read the driver's identification and memorized his number. You slumped against the back seat like a thief, keeping your chin down, your expression neutral, wondering who exactly was going to keep track of you.

⚬⚬⚬

The dog is taking the house apart. Each day you come home to find that something else has been eaten. A wicker basket, something you once made out of papier mâché, an African mask, one high-heeled shoe. You know you should be angry, these are your things after all, but you find yourself humming as you pick up the bits and scraps of knick-knacks, strangely anticipating the next casualty. You understand this anxiety, this need to strip everything bare, to rip through the sturdy right down to the essentials. Lately, your dreams have been cloudy and white, and it seems that they are of nothing, a pale milky blankness where nothing exists. If you lived without mirrors, all you might see of yourself all day is your hands, busy, using things, shaking, or just folded, quiet for a moment. In your dreams, when you look down, you do not even see your hands. You sweep away threads of a carpet you bought at a craft show, a charcoal drawing of your first well-proportioned nude, and a picture of your mother swimming, the only evidence of such a time. Your house seems to be expelling itself. Each time you look around it seems a great contraction, some kind of quake, has shaken loose your things, leaving them scattered and half-torn all around. The dog tugs a sweater across the floor; the empty arms dragging along the wood look like the legs of some strange, boneless deer and make the dog seem more savage than he really is. You ask yourself: What do I need? What do I need? But it seems that there is nothing that you miss. You love your dreams where nothing ever happens and pieces of you disappear, so that it seems that you might be becoming something close to breath.

●━●━●

In your mother's house there were many things. When you think of your mother you sometimes imagine a kind of fiendish, malignant Maria from *The Sound of Music*, spastically dancing in her little movie about love and war and gloating over her favourite things. Your mother was a hoarder. She kept her good pots and pans underneath her bed to ensure that they were never damaged or burned. She kept her favourite coffee mug, a dark-blue ceramic piece covered in little white flowers, in her lingerie drawer. There was always the fear of breaking things in your mother's house. It seems to you that after you broke a particular red glass thing, your mother began locking herself more and more in her bedroom. You remember, after your mother left, going through some of these bedroom things and finding a crayoned note with a scribbled stick figure of your mother and a red flower in a red glass vase, something that you must have slipped under your mother's door in apology that said simply: Hello, mommy.

●●●

It gets easier. At first you muffle her cries by hiding in the bathroom, the shower running hot. You sit fully dressed on the edge of the tub and let the steam smother you. When your skin is damp and your cheeks are flushed, you open the door and the air makes you shiver. You make yourself cold and ready for her. You put her down on her stomach, her forehead pressed sadly into the mattress. Sometimes her head moves from side to side, denying everything. You do not like the way she looks up at you. Her eyes are abnormally huge and she hardly seems to blink. It is the only way she has to take you in. She has not heard the sound of your voice very often. Who does she think you are? What does she know about you? Soon, it seems she does not cry as often. She is trying to frighten you with her silence. Her hands will reach out and grab hold of your finger if you tease her with it. But this is an uncontrolled movement, involuntary. Her eyes are still adjusting. She cannot make out friend or foe. She reaches for the nearest thing at hand, but it has nothing to do with closeness.

It gets easier. When you leave her now, your heart slows right down by the end of your walkway and returns to its even tapping, or something more like a drip, a kind of Chinese water torture. Inside the house, the dog rages for you. Your house frays. Seams expose themselves. Fragments of materials — bedding, covers, diapers, and all types of everyday items, pieces of plastic Tupperware, spatulas, bathtub plugs, and toilet plungers — everything, scattered in colourful chunks and pieces like confetti or rice showered at some strange ceremony.

You drink at a neighbourhood bar. Silent television screens play European soccer games and the place is filled with reggae music. On Caribbean Night, a man without a shirt on offers to buy you a piña colada but it reminds you too much of milk spittle. Everyone looks so helpless to you, and every man calls you baby. Anyone waiting at home for you, baby? Can I get you anything, baby? It seems that no matter what you do you cannot get the smell of diapers or corn starch or that powdery infant scent from your hands. When you sweat it smells to you like sour milk. Some nights you dance by yourself on a small, crowded dance floor, swaying back and forth, your body finally feeling lighter. You can feel your hip bones again as they bump accidentally against another dancer. You think that there is something right and fitting, worthy even, in taking up less and less space. One night, after you have had too much of something water-clear but potent, a man shares with you the size of his great heart. While he twirls a little mauve umbrella stuck inside his drink, he tells you long stories of all the women he has loved, and all the women he has yet to share his enormous passion with. He cannot help himself. He is filled to the brim. He orders himself another exotic drink. It is a strange bar, you think, where all the women like their shots straight up, and all the men are stirring cocktails. He seems lucky to you, this man, with his huge and generous heart. When he finally reaches out his clumsy hand and strokes your thigh, you tell him: Sorry, I am fresh out of love, and your voice sounds almost innocent, like a dairy maid, someone peach-faced, pert, and healthy. A farmer's daughter who has just run out of eggs. The man says something about fresh . . . but you are already near the door. The bartender wipes your place clean and says: Goodbye, baby.

When you turn your corner you always expect to see the red lights of fire engines or waiting police cars parked in front of your door, their mute lights spinning noiselessly, evil mimes, making the emergency seem too late. Each time, you

are surprised by the stillness of your house, the ordinary way
it sits beside the others on the block, the outside light on,
making the bright blue of the door seem rich and inviting.
It is always right here, at this moment, that you think you feel
something, a stirring, that makes you run the last half a block
and fumble a little with the keys. But by the time you reach
her, whatever it was is gone, and your heart has contracted
back down into that knotty pit at the centre of some soft
fruit. She lies in her crib with her eyes shut tight against you.
She makes hardly any noises in her sleep. Each time, you are
stunned at her determination to stay alive. It seems impossible that she willed herself here, right into this world, without
any encouragement at all. Sometimes, you just want to shake
her out of her dumb sleep, shake her and crush her tiny chest
against yours until she cries in a terrible hopeless fear. But
you grip the bars of the crib hard and hold your breath. It
passes. Isn't it better to feel this dark-pitted emptiness than
the other, the urge to damage and betray?

●➤●

There was a man, of course, with beautiful eyelashes and the
face of a drifter, a face that could be heaped up by air or
water currents and carried anywhere. He said, "I'll be back."
But it didn't matter. You never loved him, that is, not here,

not anywhere where he was with you in the same place. Not in his cramped room with the blue-painted walls and the piles of hardcover books stolen from various libraries. He was obsessed with designing the perfect world or the optimum living conditions. He drew many plans and was always talking about space. "People need their own space," he was always saying. "Crowding leads to aggression." People just need less people, you thought, and said to him: Some people need more space. Others need the entire universe. But you love him in Africa, where he wandered alone for two years, where he is now, probably, somersaulting down the desert sand dunes naked, sleeping beside the Masai. Washing his feet in day-old tea. You loved to listen to his stories, to his versions of himself in Africa, and you would put yourself there with him, as one woman he might have met in Niger maybe, someone he would have taken a photograph of and showed to you here, someone dear, uncomplicated, and far away. So you love him there, but he does not know that. There is a picture of him standing in the desert in very short shorts, bare-chested, just squinting ahead at dunes and dunes of spice-coloured sand. You like him best there, one man alone in the desert, hot and free, with none of his silly plans for perfection.

You remember holding his head against your belly, untangling the knots of his hair with your fingertips, massaging the bones of his back and shoulders. Neither of you ever ate enough. You are not soft to lean against. He said there was something about you that reminded him of camping on stony ground. Hard but worth it, something he might get used to because of other things: the night, the stars, the cold smell of moss and lake. He always talked this way just before he started leaving anywhere. Preserving you somehow. Giving himself a worldly, complicated face, a heartbroken squint that would draw women to him, to stroke his tanned forehead, to smooth him out. Stop it, you would think to yourself. There is nothing natural about me. Sometimes lying there beside him in the dark it would occur to you that you could kill someone. When he slept, you would cover his body with your own and remember stories about bear attacks; how sometimes the great animal would just lie down across the body, like a dog across his bone, and just wait, wait for the body to move again, to prove itself — that it is alive or that it is dead, but the body must prove itself one way or another. You would lie across his back, your nose pressed into his dirty hair, his breathing slow and trusting, unaware of the beast that had fallen across his back. Inside your own body, life was already starting to prove itself. You sent a letter Poste Restante to Kenya. You tried hard not to pay attention to the thing inside you, hoping he was right, that without your vital focus things would simply die or disappear. But, as it turns out, life does not need your attention at all. Only when you grew so big that your dresses swelled out like tents did you imagine him here, camping underneath you, his knife strapped to his brown ankle, listening for wildlife.

●━●━●

Your father used to say: Your mother is like a stain. The more you rub her the worse she gets. This was your most erotic and generous vision of your mother, as someone who spread herself around easily, who ate her way into people's uphol-stery and just dried there. And for a while that was the way it seemed with her, that she had dried to some horrible texture right there on her bed. She had a certain look, sprawled out like that in her long rayon bathrobe and full makeup, not so much of an actress but more like someone who would look good on a talk show – pretty enough to make some audience imagine that there was still hope left for her. Sometimes, when you moved silently into her room, and sat just right, softly, with barely an indentation, beside her on the bed, she would grab you around the waist in something that might be mistaken for a hug, and in her best Bob Barker voice, scanning crazily through the television channels, would shout: And all this could be yours, if the price is right.

The remote control disappeared the day your mother left. "I'm switching stations," was all she said, clicking the thing uselessly in the air as she walked out of the house in the early morning just as the street lights were turning off. And it was understood in the movements of your father, the way he straightened the folds she had made in the rug on her way out, smoothing the tassels with his bare feet, that he had been expecting this and was somehow prepared. You watched your father realign his world – tilting a slightly off-centre mirror back into place, moving a bowl of dried flowers a little forward on the shelf, untangling the necks of umbrellas in the copper stand – and inside your head you screamed into his dog-sad face: G'won boy. Go get her. But he did not move and it seemed to you then that he had been standing at this door for a long time, leaning just like that against the handle, so firm and dense that if you reached out a fist, say, round and solid like the inside of a bell, and punched him hard right below his ribs, he might only clang and reverberate in some horrible metallic announcement. Your mother's long coat billowed behind her, and her pumps didn't make a sound against the walkway, and you realized, with the cold morning air coming in through the door and up your nightgown, that this was the lightest you'd ever seen her, that your mother was becoming wind, just a bare suggestion or intimation of someone you once knew.

Your house is going through a kind of fall, an early autumn where everything is changing shape and colour, letting go and piling up like leaves on the ground. Suddenly it is important to understand how everything works, the actual mechanics of everything you touch with your hands and pretend to know and understand, everything you take for granted in its everyday use, because lately you get the feeling that you have been fooling yourself, faking a sort of blasé familiarity with things, everyday objects which if your life depended on it you could probably never make for yourself. There must be one thing here that you can understand fully, then maybe others will follow in a natural logarithm. It just seems so wrong to make anything a part of your life, to make anything essential, if you cannot understand it, if you do not know how it works. Life is suddenly mathematics. First you multiply. Than you simplify, reduce. You ask yourself tough questions. What is my foundation? Upon what have I built this self? What is this round wire thing hanging from my kitchen rack?

And so it begins. The toaster-oven. You don't know and so you unplug it. The glass you hold in your hand, supposedly recycled from old cola bottles – how is it made? Could you do it yourself? And the answer is no, so you leave it on the countertop, beside the wilting plant you cannot name, which grows from sunlight and water – but how exactly? Hand-painted plates, coffee mugs, aluminum foil, stuff in your fridge wrapped in plastic, made with real cheese products, everything, garlic, flour, teflon-coated pans. . . . You make a great pile. Everything must go. You pass the dog on the way to your bedroom, he is chewing on the sleeve of a good silk blouse. You pause to consider. Well, there is a worm somewhere that spins out of its mouth . . . this thread called silk . . . and then the thread . . . But when you find that you can't go on, you bend to pat the animal's thick, oily fur and say: Good dog.

●●●

When you think of it now, you are almost embarrassed by the way you bored your mother. The pathetic way you would trap her in some part of the house and with a little curtsy begin to prattle at her something you might have learned that day in drama class while her green-speckled eyes glazed with forced interest and then quickly went blank. *Ladies and Gentlemen. I will now recite for your pleasure the poem* . . . And you always knew, the moment that smile settled in the corner of her mouth like a little scribble, that you had lost her. You cannot imagine what she could have been thinking, examining her hands and nails and then remembering, looking up at you, trying to organize her face, all her strange mismatched features, into some orderly version of a delighted mother. And you knew you could have stopped, backed away, bowing gracefully and taking whatever applause was left, but in the same way as you poked and needled a swollen gum, on and on you went, almost tasting the little spits of blood in your mouth, and the awful pleasure of cornering your mother.

●●●

When you call her, sometimes you call her Baby – please Baby, please – but mostly she is just You: *Hey, you with the dirty diaper. Just who do you think you are? Who do you think I am?* And just for a kind of comic relief, so that she might understand that you do in fact know how to smile: *Just wait till your father gets home.* She can break your heart. All the power she hands you in one small fist. Animals are born almost ready to leave. They stand and drink and wobble, and soon their mothers disappear into a pack of identical-looking gazelles, let's say, camouflaged by all the other perky white tails who have turned away from their offspring. The shape of you, your cramped body, your tiny holes and escape hatches, your fragile, bony home, everything you are makes her frail and helpless. Doomed from the start. You should take her to the doctor one day. You really should. It is time. But you just can't. Once you even dress her up in a flowery spring hat and attach her to your body in one of those baby carriers with so many ropes and ties the two of you might as well be going bungee jumping. You stand at the door with your fingers gripping the handle. You just stand there. The baby falls back to sleep and you untangle her from you and put her back in her crib.

●●●

When you are a little older and your mother has been gone a safe number of years, your father surprises you one day and tells you that your mother had given away a baby girl when she was younger, before she met him, a few years before you were born. When he tells you this, you are both sitting cross-legged inside the giant basement closet, spring cleaning, though later you will be sure that all this really took place deeper into the summer because you will remember feeling so hot and, later on that night, standing outside on the balcony in almost nothing, trying to imagine your mother giving any-thing away. You remember your mother for a moment giving you an old fur wrap, something from a second-hand store, that had little hard patches, knots embedded near the skin, as though it had once been submerged in something wet and had never quite dried properly. Take it, your mother had said when she caught you hiding in her bedroom closet stroking the thing like a pet and mumbling softly: It's okay. I'm here. You took it back to your room slowly, almost backing away from your mother, still holding it out to her, ready at any moment to give it back. But it remained with you the whole day, though by the next morning the stole was back on your mother's closet peg as though it had never left. It didn't matter really. What thrilled you was the idea of your mother sneaking into your room while you slept, her perfume like a drug, covering you in a fog, a spell. Did she stop to watch you sleeping, taking note of your tiny breaths and the little whistle of air through your nose? Were your limbs exposed, did an arm or foot dangle over the side of the bed, glowing just a little from the cracked night light? Was she moved at all by your smooth child's body or your dreamy abandonment? "I'll give you something, honey, I will," your mother was always saying. "But not that." And whatever it was, it was always not that. You remember your father sitting in the mouldy closet, turning his watch around and around on his wrist, saying to you in his sad stern voice: It is important for you to know that she says she was attacked. For a long time you could not imagine what he meant and thought only that to your mother life had always been a big surprise.

●━●━●

Your home has taken a deep breath and expanded as things continue to disappear. The radio has waves and bands that you do not understand, your chair was once a tree, so were your books, your papers, your letters. Even your own photographs are mysterious to you, memories you tried to plan, but how they came to be here so sharp and glossy you couldn't say for sure. So they go. The dog is taking care of other things. A small twig chair that you thought you understood is gone, a thin wooden woman someone sent you from Zimbabwe, a long strand of fertility shells, your father's pipe, also gone. You and the dog pass each other now and again as you put another thing in the give-away box, as the dog swallows something new. You each have your ways of getting rid of everything hard and corporeal. He takes it all into himself, enfolding and engulfing each thing into his big hairy body, and you push everything away from you, thrusting. You gulp at each other, each creating more and more space for the other. The baby lies in her crib in the middle of your home, staring up at the stained ceiling while the world around her dismantles. Once, she was tightly squeezed inside you, her palms pushing up against the walls of your body, of her galaxy, snug like a star embedded in a dark sky. Now all around her only air, and a looseness, something lax and adrift, everything collapsing around her each time she reaches out a shaky fist to touch something. Sometimes when you leave the house, the dog sits staring out the window for a long time until in a panic he finds something else to destroy. You are beginning to see that there is a very fine line between solitude and confinement.

Because your mother left almost everything behind, it was not difficult to believe that she had simply cracked. It was easier to think of her that way, as someone who might have gone explosively mad, rather than as a woman fully possessed of her conscience, making her ludicrous choices with deliberate care. The pots from under her bed went back to the kitchen cupboards, but neither you nor your father could bring yourself to use them, except once, when your father made a weird, stringy chicken stew and left the largest pot of all on the stove overnight, until it smouldered to a chunky black mass that would not be cleaned. Your father's rages were minor and contained. He could focus, and like the expensive lidded pot, he could keep any mess hidden inside himself. You hate to think what has congealed at the bottom of your father. You are sure that between the two of you, you and your mother, the way you both lump and bubble, he will never be properly cleaned.

The only thing you took of hers, when it seemed that you could finally take whatever you wanted, was her black metal box with the old-fashioned key taped to its bottom. Mom's Black Box, you call it, and the image conjures up visions of your mother as the wreckage of an airline disaster, scattered all around an open field, burning out of control. Inside you expect to hear her last words, panicked or sickly calm, you cannot decide, though in either case the same words: I'm going down. I'm going down. The dog has not found a way to get inside yet; the metal box baffles him, like the ostrich eggs that confuse a pride of hungry lions. He paws at it in frustration, knocking it from side to side, but there is no soft underbelly on this thing, nothing to really sink his teeth into. What is inside the box speaks of its own disaster. Newspaper clippings your mother saved over the years and felt the need to hide in the strongest box she could find. *Born 10/09/62 St. Mary's Hospital — Am I your daughter.* Or, *Is Someone Out There Looking For Me? Please Contact.* Small, neatly cut squares from the personal columns, items that might have whispered of infidelity, of a loose and playful image of your mother you could have cultivated into a fantasy, but which instead gave evidence of an altogether different kind of abandonment. Often the cut-outs were the same, the same hopeful, dogged beseeching, as though no one were getting lucky at all, and day after day, in a kind of ritual you never noticed, your mother cut them free from their public whimpering and hid them away in her black box.

In your mother's bedroom you can remember hearing the low rumbling of your father's voice, the pauses between his sentences and breaths between thoughts that always made it sound as though he were speaking in perfect grammar, so that while you listened to him you couldn't help but punctuate along. Comma here, question mark, period, and even the colon when he was about to list. Your mother, on the other hand, hooked herself around one particular phrase and

simply repeated it in varying tones, from a falsely calm bari-
tone to a shriek. She seemed to bring just one sentence to
any given argument and play it over and over again like a
theme song, so that in your memory each incident had a
title. The "don't you say that to me" fight. The "oh, is that
right" battle. The war of "that's what you think." The very
last time they fought, you remember your father leaving the
bedroom and closing the door firmly behind him, his manner
stiff and calculated like a headmaster's. Inside, your mother
was ranting: I will not. I will not. Over and over again, sometimes meekly under her breath like a vow, and then suddenly
louder, banging the headboard or the walls with her fists. Your
father cupped your head with his hands, each big palm
holding an ear, holding all of you in his hands curved like
parentheses, while your mother practised her idiotic lines –
I will not. I will not. Even then, it must have made a kind of
sense to you that even in her fighting words, her angry refrains,
she would bequeath nothing. Except in the end, she left you
everything. To sort through, to keep or discard, just a mess
of stuff, but characteristically unplanned and disorganized,
with no intention or restraint.

The dog eats through the wires of the telephone and holds
the receiver between his paws like a bone. You bend down

beside him and whisper into his big pointy ears: Hello? Hello? You make your voice and breath reverberate like an echo and he shakes his head from side to side. Sometimes when he is sitting straight and still, the tips of his paws a little flexed, his brown-and-yellow eyes narrowing, you let him stare at you and you hold his dark gaze, and in the quiet of this strange contest you feel his wildness coming at you like advice and instinct. Do not move. Do not be moved.

●━●━●

Why? said your father, long distance. And then: Stupid. Stupid. Stupid. What could you say? You knew your father didn't trust you, that he watched you like a geologist watches a fault, looking for small disturbances in your veins that might mean something big. More than once, after your mother was gone, he found you lying across her side of the bed, or posing in front of the mirror in her torn blue kimono, repeating some phrase you might have heard her say, over and over again, amusing yourself, playing mother. *I will not. I don't think so. Get out.* Your father would look at you, plainly and without expression, and say simply: No. As though you were a dog in training. He always expected that the evenness of his voice, his firm consistency, could make you reasonable. It never worked with your mother either. One time he put his hand over your mouth, as though perhaps all you really needed to understand him was a tactile aid to go with the command, and you can remember biting down hard into his hand, the small fleshy mound at the base of his index finger right around to the front of his hard knuckle. At the dinner table you watched his hand shaking salt, gripping a fork, holding the edge of his plate, and you were mesmerized by the indentations in his skin, by the impression that you had made.

For the longest time you thought it was your mother who had not wanted you, who only tolerated the life that slipped out from her and shattered across the floor like glass – her accident. You were something your mother was always cutting herself on, or bumping her shin against. The edge of a bed, the corner of a sharp table. Now, there are those small plastic pieces to cover the corners of your pointy furnishings, to make your house safe for children. But then, nothing in her life was child resistant. Except your father. "It was me," he admitted to you finally one day. "Me who didn't think you were a good idea, me who didn't believe in having children, or believed rather that some people should not have children, should not ever cause anything to be, or to be the cause of anything." Your mother simply wanted to fix something she broke once before, to make repairs, to tighten and adjust, make firm and secure, and so you can imagine that when she left she might have thought she was a plumber just going out to her truck, someone who just went out for a moment to find a rare and tricky part and never came back. It was your father who on angrier days would growl: They fix dogs by ripping out their ovaries. Did you know that? Still, he sent you a cheque, a Snugli, a bright fish mobile, and an article about the natural instincts of female clams, cut out from some magazine.

◓◓◓

In your search for something essential, your whole life has ended up in your cramped front yard. What here is blameless? Everything has been touched by you, objects hold the traces of all your vibrations, everywhere you've put your awful hands. You remember a story about a woman who decapitated two of her children right on her front lawn. Inside her house many more children shrugged their shoulders high over their ears. The days are still warm. Bicycles are chained to the iron fences all down your block. The days are still a little too long. The baby sits in her infant carrier on your cement stairs between an old pair of roller skates and a collection of Bee Gees albums. People come by and all make the same jokes. "How much for the baby?" Sometimes they answer their own jokes, strangers playing with each other, a regular amateurs' night right on your own front stoop. "The baby's free. Twenty bucks for the carrier." "Just kidding." They laugh and pun together, various snorts at different levels, and ride away happy in this friendly neighbourhood, on their old second-hand bicycles. Sometimes the women will give you an extra smile just to make sure you are taking it well. Some have heard of fluctuating hormones before. Really, you think of yourself as the carrier, the infant carrier going real cheap, the one who seems immune to disease but can surely pass it on.

It is not an official sale. Nothing is priced. Some things you give away for free, some you sell, depending on the person. That's the way that you are. At night you can hear people or animals picking at the things you've left on the curb. During the days, you wait and watch. The ones who spend the most time milling about seem to be artists of some kind. The girls have scarves tied around their heads and wear jean overalls over printed cotton bras. They ask: Can we have this? Or this? You give them whatever they want. They pick up an old mirror frame, a scrap piece of paper, an old tasselled lamp-shade, and turn it over and over in their wondrous, practical hands. Everything they touch turns to something better than it was before. Your things are suddenly "cool," and these people can make your trash beautiful. You watch as they stuff your house into their deep canvas sacks. The dog hunches beside you; his head hangs low and saggy and the fur around his face and the tips of his paws are smeared an oily red from a tube of lipstick he ate just this morning. They walk away in their big-soled shoes with pieces of your life sticking out from the tops of their bags.

"Are you moving?" asks a neighbour, leaning over her second-floor balcony, looking down on you as you sit perfectly still on your cement stairs. It is such an incredible question that you are forced to take it apart, to dismantle it for its meaning. You feel hard, marbleised like a column or pillar. The baby is dirty and her skin is patchy and rough. You have let her nails grow into spiky rodent claws and she has scratched painful little animal tracks down her face. No, there is nothing moving about you. What you mean to say is that you haven't decided yet. Maybe, if you give it all away, free everything from your small home, you might jolt and prod all of your attachments until they fall loose like broken teeth. All these things you've tried to eat, to make a part of you, all these things you've touched and used, covered in your fingerprints, dusty with the flakes of your own skin, if you can sweep all this from you, maybe you will not be the one who has to leave. You will be the one who stays, like the dog. You will not be moved.

●━●━●

She is smeared with you. Her misshapen head, the small brown birthmark on the inside of her thigh. She turned inside you, somersaults and strange twists, and coated herself in you like breaded chicken. How will she ever get away from you like this? When you change her, you put her down in the middle of your bare room, and there are moments when you find your hands squeezed tight around her thin thighs. You squeeze until you can touch the tip of your thumb to a finger. You squeeze until you see a slight eruption in her face that might mean she will cry. You drag your hands and fingers across her small body, trying to leave clues. *I touched you here. My nails dug here. Pieces of my skin settled on you like baby powder. A slim strand of hair has fallen across your chest.*

In the park where you go to sit alone sometimes, you have seen women walking away from their children, screaming something like "That's it" or "I've had enough." The children fall to the ground and a cry moves so slowly through their bodies, undulating in every part of them, you can see the thing right below the surface of their skin, like fish rising suddenly to feed. There is nothing but the end of the world and a woman walking away. They stumble after their mothers, their arms stretched forward like sleepwalkers, or tiny monsters. And the women always turn back, always bend and open their arms, baring their conspicuous chest, their heavy longing. You are the mammal that is attracted to being the world to someone. A mother bear chases her cub right up a tree, something she would have done in a time of danger, but this time she does not call it back down. She will not let it know when it is safe again. It must fend for itself. She turns around and leaves the cub behind. A bear knows what kind of animal she is. She walks away shaking her big head from side to side. This time, *she* is the danger.

●━●

Somewhere, another girl has your mother too. Somewhere, there is an escaped sister and she is better than you, cleaner, not quite so creased from being so badly held, so badly folded. She hangs in the sun like a newly washed sheet. She is something you want to wrap yourself in and press your face against. After your mother disappeared, and you knew that somewhere there was another one like you, you found yourself giving your blood away for free. Sometimes when you sat there in the hard wooden chair of some auditorium, your easy veins giving themselves up to it, you imagined you were draining a poison from yourself and this bloodletting was your way of giving everyone permission to go. And when you got up to leave, your body slightly lighter and the back of your neck hot and damp, you would think that maybe somehow this blood would find its way to that other one, a message from your wiry veins — *I am here.* On your driver's licence you ticked off all the possible organs you could give up. And because you were not squeamish, there were many. In your most gruesome fantasies, both of you need a lot of rescuing, a lot of help. You are a natural donor. And somehow she is always saved. Other times when you think of her you imagine that she is just another thing your mother has let loose on the world. Once, you got a postcard from your mother, a museum card with a sweet madonna and child, on which she had printed simply: You'll be happy to know I've rid myself of all my demons.

For the last time, you dress the baby in something yellow and terry cloth and, picking her up off the floor, you put her in her carrier and face her towards the door, perfectly lined up on the slats of polished wood, as though there were invisible tracks, like at the car wash, or some amusement-park ride. It is time, you think, and you are so sleepy that if you lay down here in your bare house you might never get up. It is time now, before many things begin to happen. Before she lies on her back and puts her foot in her mouth. Before she starts to recognize familiar faces. Before she ever mimics you, smiles when you smile, curls her wet, soft lips when you do. You have to go now, you say to her. I'm no good. But she has closed her eyes and will not look at you. The dog waits, stretched out on the floor, his head resting on his front legs. He is still skinny, though much of your house is actually inside him. From the back, in her round summer cap and her reclining seat, the baby looks like a little astronaut pointed towards the stars, waiting. You watch her, half expecting at any moment that she will be lifted from you in a great fire, leaving you behind, scorched and amazed, while she grows lighter and lighter, solemnly giving up gravity. Her cap blows away. Her bald head is a white milky planet, a round pearly moon.

Someone told you once that you were alive beyond your control. And each morning when you wake up you find that you are breathing before you even have a chance to try it another way. Just by sheer will you cannot stop your heart. On and on it goes like some boring aunt at a family gathering. On the day you carry your mother's black box and the blue rented telephone to the curb, the dog runs out into the street and is hit by the passing garbage truck. The garbage men bury their faces in their big orange gloves. You watch from the top of your stairs. One of them leans over the animal and then quickly steps back, wiping his boots along the pavement as he does. They look around, expecting some kind of screaming at any moment. When they finally notice you, one of them steps forward and starts to come up your walk. He takes off his orange glove and tucks it under his armpit. You shrug your shoulders and say: It wasn't mine. There is no one around to verify. Somehow you sense that he expects more from you, some kind of female shuddering that might mark the passing of a life. But you do nothing. Inside the truck you can see the driver crying. They decide to take the dog away. They take off their gloves and handle him with their bare hands. They flip his body into the truck and you can see that his head is leaning against a bag stuffed with leaves. You turn away and pretend not to hear the noise of the machine as it churns and pulls everything into itself, making room for more.

❤❤❤

Now that your house is empty, your dreams are suddenly crowded and thick. In your dreams it happens this way: they surround your house and you raise your baby above your head in surrender, saying: I give up. I give up. The social worker steps forward and, rising on her petite toes, takes her from you. In another one, you exchange her quickly in some alley, like a drug deal. When she is gone you open your palm to find a round black metal ball. You swallow it, and every time you move you hear it rolling through you, tapping against your bones, ricocheting down your spinal cord, making you clang and echo with each step.

You sign a paper waiving your parental rights and your hands surprise you by shaking, undulating like great white banners of surrender. You open and close your hand in front of your child's small folded face and ask for the last time: *Can you wave bye bye, Baby?* In your empty house you fully expect to sit here, right where you are, and make yourself disappear into a place where touch isn't possible, where nothing can come leaning up against you, or accidentally graze you from behind; where there's no kneading or fumbling or accidental impact. Do not move, you think. Don't make a sound. And with this advice it is unclear if you are prey or predator. What will happen? There are so many possibilities and the imagination is always unfaithful, adulterous, and inexact with all its curving foot-paths leading anywhere. You wait in the middle of your living room, lying on the floor with your arms and legs spread out into an X, as though you were a pale painted blotch on some forest tree, a clue someone left to find their way back, something that marks a familiar spot.

THE SPIDER OF BUMBA

THERE IS A PICTURE OF you in the newspaper standing between a man and a woman who for a very short time you knew as parents. The headline reads: Whose baby is this? You are wearing checkered knickers and a jacket and a matching cap that is a little too big and droops over one eye, making you squint. You look like a quaint English orphan and you wonder if this was deliberate. Even then, it seems you only smiled with half your mouth, always keeping the moment close to neutral just in case. Just one side of your mouth lifting its lips in an obligatory salute. It is the small, puffy, perfect mouth of a child. Your parents seem regular. You feel sure that if you had stayed with them you would always have had plenty of fibre. They grip your hands tightly, stretching your arms up and between them in a little Y. They are wearing sporty clothes. They are trying to look fit.

Underneath this is a crazy picture of your real father. His hair is long and he wears a tight choker of beads. You know now that the beads are red but it is only a black-and-white photo, and his eyes do not look green but soot black, and his gold skin seems stone grey. He is quoted as saying: *If you suck the nipples hard and long enough, eventually even a man's body can learn to produce the necessary milk.* Things like this did not endear him to the public. In the picture he is doing everything wrong. He holds up his hand as if to block his face like a thief. A hand-rolled cigarette burns almost to the end between his fingers. His nails are dirty and a little too long. He is a messy man. He will always remind you of something badly scribbled. He does not look fit at all, but there is something about him that is almost more than natural.

•••

This is the only fable I will ever tell you, so listen good. Your father has you by the elbow and you face him, trying not to pull away from the pressure of his fingers, which seem to grind themselves between your skinny bones. He knows he is a man with a tight grip but can never remember to loosen up. And he is a man true to his word. Honourable. A promise-is-a-promise kind of guy. This is the only fable he ever told you. There were many lessons, but nothing you could really organize your life by.

A man sits in a cement room in Bumba, a sandy town in Zaire, on the continent of Africa. He is stuck in Bumba. The next truck out of town does not leave for many days. Everywhere is too far to walk to. When he asks about the truck, the people laugh and offer him dried fish. He teaches them to use his camera. They take pictures of him sitting in the courtyard outside his room. He shares the courtyard with a chicken, a goat, and many women who sit on low stones pounding manioc. They take pictures of the man squatting in the bushes. The man spends much of the hot days lying on his cot watching a spider make its way slowly down the stained wall. He takes a picture of the spider with his hand spread beside it to show how big it is. Its body is the size of the man's thick palm. For six days the man watches the spider make a slow climb down the wall, stopping for hours, waiting, sometimes reaching out one skinny leg to wave in the air, only to pull it back suddenly. The stillness, the hesitancy of the spider make the man nervous. At night, he wakes sometimes to shine the flashlight against the wall. If the spider hasn't moved, the man has restless dreams: the truck is never coming. He is stuck in Bumba forever. On the seventh day the man sits in front of his room in the courtyard. The day is still. Suddenly the man notices the spider crawling with purpose out his door and down the stairs, onto the red dusty earth of the courtyard. Across the yard the chicken narrows its pebble eyes and stretches out its neck like an arrow. It charges across the yard, screaming like the desert wind, and the spider is gone — disappeared inside the shrieking body of a chicken. Just then the man hears the sound of an engine and smells the diesel, heavy like a fog in the heat of Bumba.

When you were seven, your father stuck out his slender neck, aimed his pointy head, and plucked you from the children's petting zoo. There is a newspaper picture of a small, red plastic purse on the dusty ground, surrounded by food pellets and goat droppings. It is a perfect picture. Behind the purse is a wire cage, and two llamas stare out from their tangled bangs, their lips slightly twisted so that their mouths seem to make little circles like back-up singers saying "ooo." In the accompanying article it is clear that your adopted parents are demented with grief. Your mother says: I just went to get her some more pellets and . . . poof. Your father says: She loves the zoo. What kind of animal would do this? Of course this is the bold black headline. What else could it be? *What kind of animal would do this?*

What you remember about your father's car that day is very dim. The shapes of these things are seen through a squint – sometimes clearly and sometimes with great distortion. You remember a puppy named Wolf – the wiggling lure that made you follow – and a dirty blue car that smells of warm bananas. You do not remember feeling scared and your father will often remind you that you didn't cry. This is the first time that your father calls you his C.O.G.F., which he tells you means "child of great fortitude." You do not understand but you are pleased by the word "great." He is not a tall man, his

shoes have wedges which are deceptive, and he has an abbre-
viation for everything. At first you cannot imagine what he
is talking about but later you will learn: it is his code, the way
he initiates you into his life; a language or dialect that makes
you kin. All his life your father will want only to be concise,
but he will always complicate. In the car your father rips his
beard from his face and, smiling, puts it in your lap. He says:
*Look, you can cry or you can flow with it. Personally, I try to be origi-
nal. To go with the least obvious response.* You remember pressing the
sticky hair across your lips and your father's approving laugh.
Good, he says. *Lesson number one. We are all in disguise. W.A.A.I.D.*

It is easy to disappear. And to become someone else. In a
motel bathroom your father dyes your hair a bluish black and
cuts harsh bangs across your forehead. *We are family,* he says.
Flesh, blood, bone. The words make you cringe, make you think
of the dentist. It has always been that way – that the language
of the family sounds so messy, sounds like drilling or extrac-
tions. The motel diner flashes a sign that says FAMILY STYLE
RESTAURANT. You sit face to face with your father in the
booth with the sticky vinyl seats that pull at the backs of your
knees. Your new bangs feel good across your head, like a little
hood. You shake your head back and forth, feeling the new
hair against your skin like tassels on a scarf. Your father
writes your new name down on the paper placemat that says

BIENVENUE. Underneath, he writes his own name, the name he goes by. *This is who you are now.* He tears off the corner of the mat and you put the paper inside your pocket. Once, your parents gave you a little blue card to carry in your pocket in case you got lost. The first line of the card said: Hello. My name is _____ . The second line said: I belong to _____ . In thick block letters your mother printed the important information. Later, you will remember your father saying: *A name doesn't mean anything if you know who you really are. S. and S. Sticks and stones.* In the restaurant, the waitress puts her hand on your father's shoulder. This comforts you. People like him. You point to a bright photograph of a hamburger in the menu. Your father orders a B.L.T. without the B., half a grapefruit, and some F.S.O.J. The waitress looks confused and this will be the first surge of protection you will feel for your father. *Fresh squeezed,* he explains. To you he says: *In this family we don't eat the animals.*

In the motel room that night – or maybe it was not that night, all the brown-and-orange bedspreads seem to have become one – your father explains it all for you. He reads to you from magazines and articles stapled together, badly photocopied, all their pages out of order. He is full of facts. Adopted children exhibit dependency, fearfulness, a lack of self-identity. They are underachievers. They steal. They are paranoid.

They run away. He is forever concerned about your developing ego. All these things he tells you, all these things he does, are for your "developing ego." The words make you feel greasy. They sound like eggs, and roadside breakfast places with holes in their plastic-upholstered stools. Later on, when you started growing hair on your body, the word *developing* made you squirm, and your father would look at you sometimes, sadly, and say: *Sweetheart, there's just no fighting womanhood.* Your father has this idea that your mother, the woman who gave birth to you, gave you bad vibes in utero. *Look how skinny you are*, he says. *It's a sign of early trauma.* Your father spends much of his time looking for your prenatal quirks. He is here to mend. If only he could remake his whole body into the perfect water-dome of a womb. When he talks to you he keeps his hand on his belly.

●●●

Still, now, you cannot figure out what kind of an animal your father really was. When your life eventually settles into something you can remember, like dirt or sand sinking to the bottom of a glass, you can see your father in his dirty blue coveralls hosing down an elephant in that terrible small zoo, or sweeping the foil candy wrappers from the ancient orangutan's cage, shaking his head, muttering about freedom coming and which side are you on. His skinny fingers had the surprising grip of animals you never expect to have such hands – a raccoon, a beaver. His eyes could narrow and widen like any of the cats'. But his face to you always seemed shaggy and thick, like the lone musk ox you once saw in a picture, shaking his big head to the lonely tundra before him, taking the blows of the vicious wind without flinching. Just walking forward against it all. The kind of animal people like to call dumb.

There was never any word that you could call the other people and so for most of your life you just referred to them as that – the Other People. Your father called them the *yics*, drawling it out like some country insult, but what he meant was – the young infertile couple. *Poor yics*, he would say sometimes, just talking to himself. You referred to your mother as "her" and you called your father by his first name, although not his real name, just the name he was hiding under. What in life is fixed or determined? Sometimes, when you think of it now, it seems as though your life with your father was only an endless childish game – a cross between dress-up and hide-and-go-seek. Or maybe it was stranger, more daring than all that. Maybe your father was always the consummate cross-dresser, forever made up as someone else. *It doesn't matter*, says your father one night, after closing down the lights in the reptile house, now the room just the orange glow of the cage warmers. *It doesn't matter. We know who we are. The greatest gods will not be named.* Still, in a way, you knew he was always amused by names. The places you stopped to live for a month or two as he carried you across the country seemed to be chosen in a fit of whimsy, a lightness that could only be achieved with your father behind the wheel of his nondescript car and you in the passenger seat getting older every day, because as soon as the car door opened, other people came in with the air and the lying began. The last few minutes in the parked car, when other families, other people, might have been collecting their things, scooping up garbage from behind the seats, putting on lipstick or sunblock or reminding each other to behave, these were the moments you spent getting your stories right. At least in the beginning, the first thousand miles or so, because after that it seemed there was a rhythm between you, an improvisational jumpiness that made it possible for you to follow each other anywhere, like jazzy horn players, or prisoners dancing for their lives.

You remember once driving through Hope without stopping. Instead, you stop in a town one mile past Hope called One Mile Past Hope. In the One Mile Past Hope Motel you watch a television program about missing children. Suddenly there they are, the Other People, crying to the greedy camera:

We will never give up. We will find you no matter what it takes. The woman wears the soft moss-coloured blouse you used to wear as a dress when you played "the lady." Her lipstick is Plump Orange and you remember it tasting like candle wax. You are surprised by her short hair. In your memory her hair hung down her back, the colour of lions. It seems that you have confused her with the Snow Fairy at the shopping mall. Somewhere, there is a picture of you on the Snow Fairy's lap. She wears a yellow gauze dress and a shiny tiara. Your small hand wraps around her own and together you share her gold-foil wand. After that, for a long time, you only wanted to wear yellow. Somehow this became the other mother the Other People would sometimes talk about. How to keep it all together? You do not tell your father of this memory. He is always saying: *No more fantasies. No more wondering.* And hitting his chest so that his voice rattles for a moment, he says: *T.I.I.B.* He waits a moment to see if you will get it and when you don't he translates quickly: *This is it, babe.*

You find your father in the drugstore buying travel tooth-brushes and hair dye. THE BLACKEST BLACK, the carton reads, FOR THE DANGEROUS YOU. *Look,* says your father. *The black sheep of the family is the dangerous ewe.* You reach way up and pull him towards you by his leather lapel. *We have to go,* you say simply. *They're coming for me.* Your father does not doubt you. He grabs a handful of nutty granola bars and pays a lazy teenager who can watch television and punch the cash at the same time. Your father drives all through the night under one moon, everyone under one moon, and just before dawn you both fall asleep at the side of the road outside a national park, beside the empty vans and wagons of other vacationing families who are probably huddled close together inside the deep green centre of the forest, listening for bears and other sudden dangers. It is only waking up sticky and hot, your cheek branded by the car upholstery, that you think that maybe it wasn't them on TV at all. Maybe now, no one is coming for you.

In your dreams the Other People are always weeping or feeding each other food pellets from their hands. Sometimes someone puts an arm around you and you can smell perfume or sweet tobacco. In your dreams they call out a name that you do not recognize and you wonder who they are looking for because there you are standing right in front of them, but they cannot see you. One morning you wake yourself up singing "How Much Is That Doggie in the Window?" You are not lost or missing. You know where you are almost all the time. You keep the map on your lap when you drive with your father, trying to keep track of all the places you are passing through. In your dreams, the Other People still stand frozen at the zoo, their hands held out to the animals, waiting. Something has been done to them and no one has any answers. To know is everything. You think at the very least that someone should tell them that you are alive. At every stop, in every motel room, you leave a note tucked inside the pages of the black bible in the bedside drawer: *I am not dead. I want to stay with my father.* Your father is not a believer. In the motel rooms he uses the bible as a coaster for his soda or a small step to reach the air conditioner. Though one time, after too many stale donuts and flat, syrupy soft drinks, he says to you: *The difference between a mother and a father is that one of those words with a capital letter means God, and the other doesn't.*

●━●━●

You spend your first year with your father running. After that you will settle in the place with the awful zoo, but that first year is mostly highway dust and gas stations and when you remember your father then your memories are all in profile. The contour of his nose, his ruddy right cheek, his long fingers fiddling with the radio, or just resting on his knee, or sometimes absently massaging his own thigh or the back of his neck. His past is sketchy, loose and chalky like charcoal drawings. But he is fixed and persistent about father-hood. *I am not some one-night stand. I want you to know that.* You remember this moment with tenderness. He does not abbre-viate; still, in your head you repeat: *One-night stand. O.N.S.*

Now, when you think about it, it seems you should have told your father that you would never ever take advantage of him, that you were not that kind of girl. At the time, it was just one thing out of many that your father told you, and you filed it away perfectly, preparing for that day when suddenly everything would change again and someone would be gone or lost, away or missing, left behind or far ahead of you. *I was always in it for the long haul. Always.* And there it is, that dark extended hallway with so many doors leading so many places, and awful ancestral pictures hung along the walls, their eyes shifting back and forth.

Sometimes your father turns off the radio and sings, suddenly, loudly, with threatening emotion . . . *The way you haunt my dreams, no no, they can't take that away from me.* He has a serious jazz twang, this hippie who loves Gershwin. He knows how to make his voice vibrate just right, and, like everything else, he takes music very seriously. Sometimes you join him in the duet, each of you taking a word and belting it out: *No / They / Can't / Take / That / Away / From / Me!* Much later you will wonder if all of it was just some kind of live-action musical for him, if he always saw, with his clear, urgent eyes, all the theatrical possibilities you were living out. Was he real, you will ask yourself, or was he a ham? Was he a sucker for the spotlight, and did he ever love you, truly, exactly? You have an image of your father driving into a flat movie set of a pink dawn, saying: *You and me kid, we'll never be left in the dark again.* You have no idea what your father dreamed about at night.

You must master your reality, your father says, and one day drives you out to the cemetery in the next town, the one with the arched stone entrance and the greenish fountain dirty with rainwater and soaked leaves. He points to a gravestone crushed between many others and tilted slightly forward, and says: *This is your mother. She shot herself.* You cannot imagine your expression. From your father you learned how to keep your lips flat, and to stop a quivering chin by turning your eyes inwards and imagining a long, dark tunnel into yourself. It was not that you were ever forbidden to cry, only that one day your father called you his partner in crime, said it in such a way that made you never want to let him down. The late movies in the motel rooms were always about young girls running away with men that looked like your father, or were those *Bonnie and Clyde* types where two people only seemed to have each other against the world. But something must have happened to your face that day, a twitch, a bitten lip, that made your father bend to you in his wide blue jeans and brown Wallabies and hold you tight in his arms while you hung your head over his shoulder and stared down through the earth to the bones and dust of your mother. Is it possible that your father says this: *Your mother was a killer, an astronaut, a shepherd, a donut maker, a secretary, a revolutionary, a user, a nun, an innocent. She was the life of the party. She was my one true love.* For the first time your father didn't care about the truth. He would have given you anything in that moment. *I told her I was coming back. She wanted time to find herself,* he says, finally, and her lost family huddles beside her lopsided headstone and she is still nowhere to be found and right beneath their feet. Sometimes, to comfort yourself at night, you choose not to believe him. It is your only secret.

You spend most of your time with your father at the zoo. When you are not watching him clean or hose down the animals, you and your father lean your foreheads up against the cages and he teaches you everything he knows about the animal. In some other place he studied wildlife biology. In some other time he was going to do something great for the animals. Here, he keeps his head down and sweeps and tries hard not to talk smart. It is the only place your father is truly quiet. You can tell that some people feel bad for you. From the outside your life looks very small. The zoo lets you wear blue coveralls and a cap that says DON'T FEED THE STAFF. In the summertime when the place actually has enough visitors to warrant turning on the cotton-candy machine, you put on big rubber boots and spend the afternoons throwing pieces of fish to the sea lions. Sometimes when you walk across the grounds from the reptile farm to the African jungle you hear the visitors mumbling: This is the worst zoo I've ever seen. And it is true. Over half the cages are empty, but there are still signs misleadingly placed across the bars: THIS ANIMAL BITES or DANGEROUS CARNIVORE, and bits of other animals' droppings, dogs', goats', dried elephant patties, placed here and there to make the cage look lived in. Sometimes someone, a mother or father, stops you to ask if there is actually an animal in there. Oh, yes, you answer in your most official voice, and the lies come easily now. *The animal is painfully shy. The animal is in mourning. The animal is feeding. The animal is playing hide-and-seek. Oh, can't you see it? There's its snout.* You are amazed at how long people will stand at an empty cage, hope keeping them there like hunters, quieting each other with expectant *shh*s, waiting. When you see children lost, crying and turning in circles, cotton candy hanging from their sticky little hands, you do not know what to do. Most of the time you walk away.

What does it mean to be nine, to be ten? What does it mean to be a child, with all the energy and fidgety pep of other children? When you are at school you are quiet and reserved. You do not have any friends but it is not because anyone is cruel to you, only that you cannot bring yourself to belong to anybody else. When you walk home from school down the quiet tree-lined streets, or out on the narrow old highway that leads out to the zoo, you imagine that you are the only person left on earth, the last of your kind, wild and unprotected. It seems impossible to you that at one time you were afraid of the dark. When was that? You can remember clinging to the Other People from nightmares. All your life you knew someone was coming for you. Now, you imagine that no one needs you. No one thinks of you and is hopeful or despairing. You are not the reason for anything. If you went extinct now, no one would care. At one time you did not know what you were going to be, growing there in the dark of some now-dusty womb, and yet you were already yourself, already packaged and ready to go. You lose yourself the minute you are born. The world calls dibs. At the zoo, your father makes a stuffed mother for the orphan howler monkeys. They hang on to its upholstered body and try to feed it fruit mash. You have never seen anything sadder. Each time your father passes the cage he shakes his head and mutters: *Motherhood.* It is part envy and part disgust.

●━●

Years pass with your father, each one more amazing to believe – is it really that easy to disappear? – and in this time you only see your father kiss another woman once. She is the "human interest" woman from the local newspaper and she is doing a story on the tragedy of the zoo. Pages of her newspaper line the wild-rabbit hutches in your backyard. The dog finds the babies in the stretches of field behind your house, or people bring them to you, feeble unlucky rodents uprooted by the weed whacker or other mechanical lawn work, their mothers gone, road accidents or owl kills. You try to keep their bare worm-coloured bodies warm and you and your father take turns feeding them from droppers. The ones that live are released. Mostly, you bury the fetal bodies in a corner of the yard, drowned by too much milk or dead from hopelessness in your pink scaly hands.

You hear voices in the kitchen one night, your father's voice so low you almost do not recognize it. It is the first time you have ever heard him whisper. From the dark hallway you can see your father slumped in a kitchen chair, his hand firmly wrapped around a beer bottle. The woman stands beside him, her bare thighs leaning against the old wood table. Oh, she is saying, you've been to Africa. Your father does not look up at her when he talks. Only the little light over the stove is on and the room smells like beans and burned rice. The woman lifts your father's face in her palm and you can see that he is resisting slightly, pushing down against her hand, by the way the folds of his skin turn up over his chin. She leans down to kiss him, and her dark, straight hair covers his head and shoulders in a cape. From where you are standing you can see your father's hands close around her back and the way his nails dig into the fabric of her dress. And then in a moment your father's hands are pushing her away and he buries his head in his arms on the table, his shirt sleeves rolled up over his muscles almost to his shoulders. The woman does not know what to do. She twirls a strand of your father's hair between her fingers. You step into the kitchen and in a strange voice say: *You'd better go now.* Soon the back door slams and your father raises his head. You stand beside him and sip his beer. He says something in Latin and translates for you. *Post coitum animal triste est.* After intercourse the animal is sad. It is the first thing your father ever taught you about sex.

●●●

You cannot be surprised. Really, it seems you should have been filled with panic and dread in such a restless world, where all the events in your life were so unpredictable. And yet, even now, there is very little that can make you jump. Your father's words: *Don't be too attached to any place. Don't be too attached to your hope.* And more important: *Wipe that kidnapped look off your face.* Later on, doctors will try to coax you. They will ask you if you feel powerless. They will ask you if you feel frightened. Maybe there should have been more conflict, deep troubled nights, awful anxious clashes, but you cannot seem to come up with very many, no matter how hard you are probed. When you think of your father you mostly think of long nights, years that seemed like a vigil or a wake where you sat up with the body, kept your eyes wide and aware, just to keep his strange, betrayed soul company.

So after seven years with your father you are not at all surprised when two men appear at your front door, and, flashing badges with a flick of their thick wrists, insist that they have found you. They ask you your name. They show you a picture of the Other People and ask you if you recognize them. It is an old photograph. You are standing beside them on the beach in front of a fried-clam stand. You are clowning, and wear the sand pail on your head like a little soldier. It is strange, but in the photograph you recognize everyone but the child. It is an odd picture to have chosen for such an occasion. What could anyone have been thinking of, except perhaps reminding you that before all this, really, your life was a gag, a perky vaudeville, a real good time. They ask you if you know where your father is. It is difficult to understand from all their questions who is lost. The light outside is strange. Not quite dark enough to turn on the orange porch lamp but not quite light enough to see clearly what is happening.

And deceit is everywhere. Scientifically speaking, the sky is everything but this odd fire-blue. It absorbs all the wavelengths of colour except the one it is reflecting. It is named exactly for what it isn't. Your father is a wanted man, says one of the detectives, and pours a package of Chiclets into his mouth. You wonder, what does it mean to be wanted? Your father has explained himself to you many times. *It is important for you to know that you were wanted, that you were never abandoned, that I never surrendered you to anyone.* Desires are strange. It is difficult to know precisely the desires of these men on your porch. We want you to come with us, says the one with all the gum in his mouth. You will be safe. And there is your father in his dirty blue coveralls, walking up the sidewalk, getting closer to your walkway, and he sees you leaning against the door, the men big like columns beside you, and for a moment you think maybe he is going to run, but he does not slow his pace, he walks steady and sure, right to the waiting men. How easy it is to switch from wanted to wanting. The detectives close their bodies in front of you like sliding doors. He has the right to remain silent but on his way to the dull undercover car he says to you over his shoulder: *S.O.B.* You nod to him, you like him defiant, but he is not saying what you think he is saying and it has been such a long time since you have misunderstood him. *Spider of Bumba*, he says, and turns away. And in the awful slump of your father's body you see for just a moment his surrender. They put you in another car and for a while the cars drive side by side and you are watching your father's profile again, and the curl of hair that has fallen in front of his eye that he cannot lift a hand to move, and for just a moment this is nothing at all, nothing has happened, you are simply on the road again between towns.

●●●

This is what your father says at his trial: *The double-wattled cassowaries are New Guinea's largest land animal. Males in this species incubate eggs and raise chicks with no help from females, thank you very much.* There are many things your father could say that might impress the jury, but this is not one of them. You watch your father in the courtroom and you wonder: Well, what kind of animal is he now? He has the look of an orangutan, with his rust-coloured jacket and his long arms that dangle over the stand. He looks caught and a little bored and the whole room stares at him as if waiting for him to do something intelligent. One time he was a free man in Africa. He had days to wait for broken-down buses and he had the strength to push a Jeep from the muddy unpaved roads. He was a game-park warden, his skin was always burned gold, he'd seen a rhino give birth. Women fell in love with him. Tourists took his picture, one foot up on the thick Jeep tire, the muscles in his thighs perfect. While you were being born, he camped inside the park under a mosquito net and listened to the breathing of lions. Nobody told him. How was he supposed to know? The lawyer tilts back on his shiny heels and asks your father just what exactly it is that he does. Your father rises to his feet and sways from side to side. The room jumps a little. He really is an animal. *I'll tell you what I don't do,* your father bellows. *I don't exist to serve the infertile. I am a father.* Really, he is beating his chest. *Why doesn't that mean anything to anyone?*

When they finally put you on the stand the lawyers are all very curious to know if your father ever brought any other young girls home with him. They ask you more than once if you are sure. They take blood from you and your father to prove his paternity. In the hubbub of the clinic and the general giddiness of the people around you, for one moment when the needle is piercing its way into your skin you imagine that you are getting married. The thing about your life now is that things are inconclusive or inadmissible. There is no hard evidence of his paternity, and cryptic letters from your mother are considered vague and inessential: *Come home. Come home. There is something you should know. This free love is something we cannot afford.* Everything comes down to evidence — the grounds for knowing and believing in something. But you are not enough proof, just something found at the scene of the crime, bagged and dusted for prints. What do they mean, It is important to act in the best interest of the child? This is the mantra, the paradox. Someone will first have to define *act.* It is difficult to assess who exactly is impersonating the child. The lawyers stamp their polished shoes and twirl about in their long black robes. Your father cries and spits and runs his hands through his electric hair, making a shaggy halo around his head. The judge slams his little hammer up and down and tells your father to control himself. He confesses to your father with manly confidence but in a passive voice filled with self-restraint: I am a father too. In a terrible but predictable split second, your father grabs the judge by the silly white bow around his neck and shakes him back and forth. *Oh yeah?* he says, his wild ape body shivering. *Where's your fucking evidence, you F.A.?* Fascist asshole, you translate to yourself as they take your father away in handcuffs. You cannot imagine it, but you are laughing. Everything about him is inconceivable. And even if he is not who he says he is, whose family is irrefutable? Who does not need some proof, some corroboration?

●━●━●

Most of the pictures you have of your father are black-and-white newspaper shots. He does not photograph well. It is as though the camera can only capture his energy, leaving his face blurry and distorted or somehow warped and crooked. Your father could not believe in photography. *A picture misinterprets everything. Moments should be free, not captured.* Your father believed in everything wild and yet here was the world accusing him of kidnapping, of seizing by force, of holding captive. Some people call it snatching, a horrible word that sounds like an invasion or a pornographic movie. To your father it was always self-evident that he could not take what he never gave up in the first place. In the photograph he wears a tie-dyed T-shirt that says I AM RESPONSIBLE. The newspapers call him a hippie, a drifter. *I am not some artificial inseminator,* your father tells a journalist. *I am the real thing. I am the father. The meaning of the F-word.*

☙☙☙

The neediness of adults makes you dizzy. The first time you see the Other People again it seems to you that they are melting. Their faces seem too wet, their features thawed into a kind of watery mess. They struggle to find one expression that will not leak into another. It cannot be that you are crying. Only they are blurry, cracking and unfreezing with every minute. The man bends down on his knees to see you but he does not realize how tall you are now and he has bent too low. He crouches and his eyes are level with your chest. He stares at the pocket of your shirt for a moment and lifts himself up again. He seems frustrated with the height of everything: now he is too tall and so he bends a little at the knee, shifting his feet as though he were ready to spring. He seems to want to look you in the eyes. There is nothing to say. It is like meeting babysitters again after years have passed. Remember me? I babysat you once. You set my sweater on fire. Remember?

The woman is beginning to come alive. Her mouth is moving and you see that her lipstick is not the fruit colour you remember. It is pinker. The colour of a slap. And her scent is different, more herbal, and you are surprised that she ever did something as extraordinary and regular all these years as choosing a new perfume. Later, you will learn that during this time she has somehow managed to have a daughter of her own, which only confirms your suspicion that family is a tricky and shifty thing. At the courthouse, in a small room with muddy-green carpets and vending machines that all flashed OUT OF ORDER, the woman puts her arms around you and inhales deeply, her nose stuffed into the tangle of your hair. She is trying to find a familiar scent, the powdery smell of fine child's hair, the candied smell of breath, cheeks that smell of sun and arrowroot. But you are much oilier now and smell of the cheap drugstore perfume you borrowed from the social worker. We missed you, says the woman. But can it be that this is what she really says, or is it something else, something you will not remember? You are instead thinking like him, thinking like your father, riffing on all the ways you have been missed, as though you were a fumbled ball, a failed shot, a game that went to the other team for a while. You are such a different you, it's hard to know exactly who they mean. What is sure and fixed? After so much time, does anyone actually know who they are talking to? Aren't we all strangers every time we meet? Your social worker leads you out of the courthouse, down the wide great stairs that make you feel righteous and innocent each time you pass this way. Cameras and news people follow you. You feel the pressure of your social worker's hand between your shoulder blades, your wing bones, you used to call them. She is a "reunion specialist." She tells you when to say hello and when to say goodbye.

You have a few of your father's belongings, though the more you examine the things the more you think that maybe they are just his longings and have nothing at all to do with property. Mostly what you find are zoology textbooks and old *National Geographics* and then stacks of odd papers and books on childhood and adoption. Inside these books he has underlined and circled and written in the margins and sometimes straight across the page in various colour pens. There are matchbooks with the names of towns you passed through and a box of red hair dye that neither of you had to use. Inside a brown envelope with an X crayoned across it is a photograph of someone who might be your mother. She is leaning against a tree, her head tilted to one side so that her long thin hair falls across one eye, and she is smiling that strangely familiar half-smile with just one side of her face. When you look at this picture you lift your mouth into that same sly and noncommittal gesture and you can almost feel the rough uneven tree bark against your back. She rests one hand against her jeans and she has tied a red bandanna around one of her legs. The other hand she holds up in a lazy peace signal. There is another photograph of a woman who is probably not your mother, a blonde in Africa surrounded by village children. She wears a silly pair of khaki shorts that are too big for her, and a matching shirt tied at the waist. And finally, a note in looser woman's script, loopy, curled, and exaggerated, so that every letter looks a little like a treble clef. You assume it is from your mother, and though you have never heard her voice, she is like a tone in your mind, a pitch or timbre that you can distinguish from all other things that are not hers. It says:

> In this world, the great charade is that everyone goes around pretending as if nothing has happened.
> Well, I have happened to you.

●━●━●

After, you can never bring yourself to fake anything. It is as though you are allergic, and great red patches appear across your cheeks and forehead, like tribal war-paint or mysterious ghost slaps. You notice that people are afraid to ask you questions. Even in sex, where the patches do not matter, where they could be misconstrued as passion, you are blunt and unforgiving. In the house where you live with your foster parents they do not make-believe that you are their own. They do not try to win you over or make you call them anything special and you treat them just like colleagues, though what any of your jobs are is unclear. You sit around the kitchen table chatting as though it is the office water cooler. Their young son calls them your "frosty parents" and in the winter you help him build sloppy snowmen with bland vegetable faces, and males and females are distinguished only by the size of their icicle nipples. You try to live a normal life. You sit in your room and study biology. You are way ahead of your class. While they examine and dissect the fetal pig you feel ready for much bigger things, a human maybe. You read about cell division and think of your father.

Your father writes you strange letters from prison. He tells you that he has put your picture up on his cell wall. Even now he lets you in, he lets you know that you may permeate his life. You cannot imagine what picture it could be. You never took any photographs, you never organized your memories. Probably it is some newspaper clipping, a photo where you didn't play the coy witness, where you didn't try to hide your face, but stared straight into the wide lens without blinking. *Dear daughter, How goes your post-snatching adjustment?* He is a model prisoner. He is appealing for a more extensive library. He writes: *I imagine I will see you soon. I imagine it all the time. Prison is a kind of zoo, but I'm sure you know that already. I no longer abbreviate. I guess I will be here a long time. If you want to send me anything I could use a warmer sweater. Is it very cold where you are?* Over time you will come to believe that everyone's past is a kind of catastrophic ice age. No one is ever born at the right time or to the right people.

For now, you work at a centre for rehabilitating wild animals. You know how to hold a loon and a Canada goose. You put soft elastic bands around their beaks to keep them from poking you. Sometimes you sleep with another volunteer, an ornithology student with the flat, pale face of a snowy owl and a way with the raptors. It seems that all the people you sleep with hate their parents and this is what they like to talk about afterwards. You lie beside them and think very bold and insightful things. How neat it is for you, how perfectly orderly, that your mother is packaged in a box underground and your father is trapped in a clean square cage. And all the others, parents and guardians, dismissed like servants, or rather, filed away in a most precise system under the tag of "helpful hints" — like tying your shoelace, printing your name, or how to say hello to strangers, and how to live with other people, share their glasses and other stuff, and avoid the back-wash of their ruined love.

●━━●

On the day your father finally gets out of prison you will take him to your apartment where you imagine you will be able to feed him and act grown up. But he will be restless. He will throw all the pillows off the couch like an old dog trying to get comfortable. He will flip through the television stations. Finally, he will go out for a walk and he will stay out all night. You will be taller than him now and the first thing he will say to you is: *You look like your mother.* Or maybe not. Maybe you will pick him up in front of the prison gates in a rundown Volkswagen, your hair long and wild and dyed an outrageous blond. You will give him a pair of faded second-hand Levi's and a freshly washed jean shirt and he will change in the cramped back seat of the car while you watch him, his prison-pumped chest, in the rear-view mirror. This time you'll do all the driving. People at the motels will mistake you for a couple. Or maybe you will disappear and he will find only an empty apartment and a box of his things. Maybe you will leave a picture of yourself on the bathroom mirror. Will he try to find you again? Maybe this time you will not give yourself up so easily. You will play the hard-to-get daughter. You will flirt with the idea of family but you will never really follow through. Certainly you must take precautions. Somewhere you learned that family is what happens to you if you don't use protection. What you mean is: there are so many sad grown-ups – how will you care for them all?

MOTHER: NOT A TRUE STORY

MOTHER (NOT HER REAL NAME) stands in front of the door. Her palm is flat against the frame and she can still feel the slight vibration from the slam. A second sooner and it would have caught her in the face, or worse. Too bad really. Physical pain is nothing compared to what goes on in the head, she sees that now; how bloodless, clammy shock, the burn of open, unprepared skin, or that thumping blue of throbbing, is the best, most benevolent diversion of them all. It pulls everything away from meaning (and all its mean intentions) right down to the very centre of unashamed survival. (She could go for a knife wound right now. Yes she could.) And if, say, her fingers had been caught in her daughter's door, crushed by her explosive, petulant slam, maybe then her daughter might have heard the surprised whimpering of her mother, might have come and knelt beside her against the wall, and whispered, horrified with grief, "Oh mother, oh mother," and run for ice and bandages and held her hand with tenderness and awful remorse. Chances are, though, she would have been only disgusted and more hardened, bare, palpable weakness kindling her anger. So Mother stands with her hand against the door and she sees that she can trace the name of her daughter where the old wooden letters of her name have been pried away after years. She tries it with her eyes closed and she can almost make the whole name out, drawing her fingers along the rough, sticky patches that will not peel away. Childhood is like that really; a thing outgrown and stripped away, like posters, stickers, memorabilia, but forever traceable by its gluey, mean patches. And anyway, didn't there used to be a rule about slamming doors in the house, probably, but that was a long time ago, long before her daughter started smearing dark charcoal under her heavy eyes so that she looked like a frail, anemic football player, and before Mother started finding disturbing little lists in her daughter's handwriting that said only: *Lunch — 1 Melba toast. 1 cup hot water.*

And what was that other thing the mother used to say long ago when things were disintegrating badly, when, say, her daughter started that terrible rodent squeaking that heralded stormy weather, seismic temper tantrums, and the end of the

world? Oh yes, something she read in a parenting book once
and underlined in sea-green crayon. "Use your words." Would
it be too late now to whisper through the seams of the door,
"Use your words now, honey"? She hears the refrigerator
humming downstairs and she sees the room at the end of the
hall, the guest room, where her husband finally tried to die
two years ago while she pounded miserably and ambivalently
on his chest so that he died in the ambulance instead. Standing outside her daughter's room, surrounded by her house,
she pays close attention to the eddies of her mind, the backwards circling of her wishy-washy thoughts, and she finds that
as usual lately she is thinking two distinct things at once:
Head high and pull up your socks, and, Life is treacherous;
comfort is impossible. This thing, this being of two minds
all the time has been getting worse and worse, becoming a
sort of obscure Tourette's or magic spell where she will say
and then un-say everything she has said. And now, why had
her strange mind alluded to the eddies of her thoughts? Her
husband's name had been Eddie. In this same way, over and
over again, everything is both interesting and dull.

She calls her daughter's name, now, according to her daughter, not her real name at all. "Go away," she hears from inside
the room. Her daughter's voice sound muffled, gagged almost,
and she pictures her head wrapped in the pillow like a gun in

a silencer. "You are not my mother." Zing. Mother presses her forehead against the door and forgets to dodge the bullet.

It hurts, it really does, then she is surprised to find that she is sickened with the unoriginality of it all, its derivative TV quality, the oily, seeping tragedy that is her teenage daughter. She remembers a friend in New York who after so many years was finally mugged, and the way this friend described how beneath her conspicuous pounding heart was another sensation, one not all that far away from boredom, and there was this repeating refrain in her head: Not this? Not really this?

❧

"Of course it's just a phase, a developmental spurt, a perfectly predictable pass," says Mother's friend Will, who lives on the second floor of their shared triplex. "Adolescents are gritty and fine at the same time."

Mother listens to Will because he is a social worker at a centre for juvenile offenders, but she cannot completely believe him because he has no children of his own. What does that mean really, wonders Mother, *of his own*? Her mind is furiously precise with these clarifications and qualifications, of all her thoughts, of all of language. What she means, she explains to herself as though she were translating for an alien visitor, is that

Will, though he cares for many children, does not keep any in his domicile, nor has he raised one from a baby. There.

Mother listens to Will drone on about the theories of rebelliousness and she feels herself growing sleepy with impatience. Her eyes burn from trying to stay wide and open. She counts the seconds between her blinks. When, she wonders, did this happen? When did her dear friend Will become so dull and so stupid? Some layer of manners and gentility is peeling away from her horribly, and suddenly she is warped. All the heaviness in the world, all the weight of everything put together could not flatten or repair this curled edge that is starting to come loose. She tilts her head from side to side trying to find the right position for her cranky, thin neck. Over Will's head she can see a mirror, and tucked into the corner of the mirror she can see his cherished greeting card. She knows it well and she has fingered it many times, smiling kindly. It is from a former lover (artsy but faithless, was how Will described her), who painted a quick splish-splash watercolour of a beloved island in Algonquin Park (Oh, that island, she has heard Will sigh; oh, the spontaneity) and inside the card is penned that weird little line that aches to this day to be a palindrome: *Will I love you I always Will.* Silly, thinks Mother. Lately, she wants to crush it, crush it right before his disbelieving eyes, these things that people keep, these things that people keep for keepsakes.

Mother tells Will, "It's different now. It's different now because she is saying things like 'I want to find my birth-mother.'" Mother says this and feels so many things at once that she actually has to grab the edge of the table for support, otherwise she might fall over. Her voice catches like a thread in her clothing and begins to unravel. She is speaking forward but her voice is coming up out of her like a thing in reverse. First, she says, "It must be terrible not to know where you come from. Just awful. Awful of mythic proportions, if you know what I mean." And then she says, "Birthmother. What kind of stupid-ass word is that? I know what it means and yet it sounds like such a fake word, something made up, like those sloppy politically correct words that exist just to make a fool of you, so unmelodic, so unharmonious, so stuck in your throat you practically choke on them."

"*You* practically choke on them," says Will.

Will thinks Mother uses the second person too much, always telling everyone how they feel when she is of course actually describing herself, never owning her own emotions, using, as Will might say, the language of blame to express her shameful heart. Once, Will said to Mother, "I can't express to you the freedom I feel when I use the first person," and Mother's thoughts, which had been at the time preoccupied with her husband's sickness, turned to her friend Will whom she saw suddenly in his bad kitchen light as a sadist, using and abusing all sorts of people. Will is a persistent and permanent friend. He is still trying to teach Mother her lesson and his voice is almost school-marmish. He is teaching her all about "I" messages and he flutters his lashes at her to entice her to smile, but with his long, grey, stringy hair pulled back at his nape and his round, dainty glasses, he looks instead to Mother like a frisky spinster. He is saying, "When we use 'I' statements we are saying, 'Look, this is a feeling *I* am experiencing. It's my feeling and it isn't something you have done to me.'" But what if it is, thinks Mother. What if you feel done *to*? How do you express that? Which person could best express that for you?

"Is that what you do all day long? Correct people?" Mother asks Will. Her voice is cranky and crisp. "Is that why they call it a correctional home under the Department of Corrections? Young offending Johnny says, 'I want you to fucking go to hell' and Will says, 'Good "I" statement Johnny, but next time don't split your infinitive like that.' Is that really how you spend your time?"

"Oh," says Will, hurt but trying to rise above it. "Just say, 'I'm sad.'"

"Okay, you're sad," says Mother. "You're obviously very sad."

•━━•

This feeling of being about to fall over, it is with her so often now she finds herself noting those things she can grab on to, the way a claustrophobic might mark an exit sign. A lamppost over there. A column in the middle of the room. These armrests right here. Here is a man's hand and a woman's shoulder bag.

She has only really blacked out once, conveniently in the doctor's office, when he announced to her husband that his melanoma was aggressively spreading and there wasn't anything to be done any more. Yes, Mother is remembering how she heard the words as though her eyes were closed, and how the voice that was coming at her sounded as though it were coming through a megaphone, or down a long, long tunnel, or through the piping in some very old house. One minute she was holding tight to her husband's hand and stroking his almost hairless wrist with her long smooth fingers, and the next minute she was staring up into his stricken face and the doctor was saying, "Upsy-daisy."

Over and over again she replays this scene in her head, mortified at her awful hogging, her show-stopping melodrama. "Not everything is about you," her daughter spit at her in a surprising fury once, surprising because it was so unlike her polite, sober daughter. And what was that all about again. Ah, yes. A sleepover at someone's house, *with boys*, and Mother had said something prissy and old-fashioned about guarding the reputation of the family, something quaint and silly like that. But that was before, before she realized just how carefully you have to choose your battles.

She imagines again her husband, blanched and clammy, reaching out for her as she slipped away and down underneath the doctor's desk, scraping her forehead along the sharp wooden edge. She sees the way he held the wad of Kleenex to her bleeding head and actually smiled at her, his lips barely parting, his eyes trapped in a wince.

On the way home in the car she said, "Upsy-daisy? What kind of world-renowned oncologist says 'Upsy-daisy'?"

Her husband was quiet for a long while and Mother thought about the way she was driving, how here she was, a woman who always waited for the door to be opened for her and never ever used a self-service station, here she was speeding down the road, barely stopping at the stop signs. And then she heard her husband say quietly beside her, "Upsy-daisy. Pushing up the daisies. Daisy, daisy, give me your answer true." Mother pulled the car over to the side of the road, her hazards blinking on and off, two little green arrows on the dashboard pointing impossibly in two directions at once as Mother's head began to split, and they held each other and cried and cried and still she remembers that she stopped crying first.

- - -

It is evening, dark, spooky October, and leaves scuttle and scratch along the pavement like claws, or whip suddenly around the corner like spies. Mother kicks at them and they scatter. She pushes open her door, shoving slightly with her hip, and is relieved to find that her daughter is not there. If she has to listen to Eric Satie one more time, she knows, she will scream, or maybe not scream, maybe simply dissolve, melt to a heap of clothing like the witch in Oz. With Satie echoing through her daughter's room, the house takes on the aura of a foreign film. Her daughter is so lovely and pouty. She, the mother, looks so much younger than she is. Everyone is caught in so much reverie that their faces might as well be windowpanes foggy and smeared with rain. Just last night, she sat with her daughter at the kitchen table, a steaming pot of tisane between them, forcing memories at each other like poisoned food, each waiting for the other to go first and swallow.

"Tell me again," said her daughter. Her thin, fine hair was just washed and still damp. She twirled it in sections with one finger, leaving long, thin noodley coils around her head.

"Well," began Mother, "Like I said before. We met the social worker at the end of a far-off corner of the hospital parking lot. We weren't allowed inside the hospital and she handed you, all wrapped in a blanket, to us, to me actually, and I was worried that I would drop you, I was shaking so hard, shaking and . . ."

"What colour was the blanket?" asked her daughter, interrupting, impatient with Mother's drama.

"White, I think, or I don't remember. Maybe pink?"

"The hospital just gave you the blanket like that, as a gift?" Her daughter's eyes were, as they say, piercing.

No, no, no, thought Mother. I never did anything to deserve those eyes. "I don't know," said Mother. "I guess they did. Why? What are you getting at?"

"It's just that it seems a bit strange that the hospital would be giving away their blankets like that, strapped for cash as they are, it's hard to imagine that you get a free blanket with every baby."

"So maybe we brought the blanket from home. Maybe they told us to bring a blanket. It's so hard to remember, honey. I know it seems that it should all be crystal clear, a pristine and preserved image, but it isn't and I don't know what to say."

"Maybe the blanket was from my birthmother." She watched her daughter steady herself against the word, the way you might ready yourself to speak the names of genitals aloud, with extra force and conviction as though they were just any old words. Mother remembers learning to smoke in the mirror the same way. Practised casualness. Studied la-dee-da. "Maybe," said Mother. "I never thought of that."

"Did you keep the blanket?"

Mother shook her head. All of a sudden she couldn't really remember if there ever was a blanket. Maybe they'd just handed her daughter to her, jerking and naked. Maybe she'd just shoved her under her trench coat like a stolen statue and run.

"What about a bottle? Did they give you a bottle of formula to take with you?"

Mother wrapped her hands around the teapot for warmth and kept them there, pressed hard, even though they were almost burning. She was testing herself. What could she stand? "I can't remember. I guess they must have. It would make good sense." Mother stopped abruptly and bent her head. Why had she said that thing about good sense? Her daughter would not be so gentle with her now.

"Yes, I guess it would make good sense. It would also make good sense that my original name was probably on that bottle, if, say, they had had the good sense to take it from the nursery, where surely I was known as someone other than 'baby girl.' And it would also have made good sense for me to have had a hospital bracelet, don't you think, because even though I was slated for the give-away bin, chances are there were rules about identifying the babies in the hospital and all that. It would, after all, make good sense."

"I can understand how angry you must be and I can see how much this hurts you," said Mother, secretly pleased with all her "I" messages.

Her daughter glared at her and said, "I talked to a search consultant who said that pretty much every time, adoptive parents are hiding something."

Search consultant? What an odd, improbable term, something like talent agent, thought Mother. Just a few months ago Mother had found a list of all the boys her daughter had a crush on, alphabetized and marked with squiggles and underlines, pasted inside her daughter's closet. And now search consultants? Everything about her daughter's life seemed suddenly to her so very frightening and perverted.

"Honey," said Mother evenly. "If you want to find your," and here she faltered only for a second, "origins, I have always given you carte blanche."

"Yes you have," said her daughter, pushing herself up quickly from the table. "But what does carte blanche mean? It means basically 'blank card,' empty space, white nothing. That's not exactly the same as help, is it?"

Later, Mother sat beside her daughter on her bed. She had come to tell her daughter that she would never hide anything from her, that she would never lie to her, no matter what anyone else might say. She had come to explain to her that, really, adopting her daughter was like winning a secret lottery, as though someone had pressed one million dollars into her hands and said, It's yours if you just shut up, and she was so afraid of making a mistake, of making anyone angry, that she did shut up and she shut her mind up too and that was how someone could wilfully forget important and impossible things. This was what she had come to say, even though she knew it would be so unsatisfying, and instead she found herself saying this: "You know, something that you said tonight jarred me, and all of a sudden I had this image of myself standing in the parking lot and looking away from the social worker for a moment, and away from you still in her arms. It seemed to be taking forever for her to hand you to me, and I was thinking this and feeling shaky and impatient, so I looked away and fixated on the hospital doors, and on a woman in a wheelchair who was squinting at me, her hands shielding her eyes from the sun. In my memory she wears a pale-blue jacket and a flowered skirt that touches her ankles, and her brownish hair is pulled back in a clip or an elastic, and at the time I remember being sure, but of course how could I know, that there was your biological mother. And then the social worker put you in my arms and there was nothing else. Nothing at all." There. She had done it. She had come in to say how she could never lie and then she had.

Her daughter's eyes seemed shiny now, clear and extra green with tears. Was it true that she was so easily fooled and persuaded, her sixteen-year-old baby, her only lasting love? She lay down beside her girl and felt her daughter relent and let her mother hold her until her breathing shifted to sleep. And Mother lay there and realized that, in life, there was no reason why things had to just happen to you. You don't have to lose everyone all at once if you don't want to.

●—●—●

"I was short some eggs," is how she used to put it, might even put it now, jokey, easy, unwilling to allow real sadness to interfere with her narrative, with making a real short story short.

It was a way, obviously, of keeping to herself, but also of not wanting to take up too much space. She pretended to be a positive person, because in the end, positive was shorter and more to the point, it packed more meaning. "Smile and the world smiles with you," she would eventually sing to her daughter as a lullaby, and that was the closest she would come to touching her own sadness, the nearest she would allow herself to buckle under the weight of all her disappointments, because if you really think about it and sing it right through, that's a very sad song. So. "I was short some eggs," is how she used to put it, "which are a key ingredient to the recipe, as it turns out," she would finish, blinking.

They tried for many years, she and Eddie, and she had two miscarriages and then they stopped trying and went to Europe for a few months, just when all their friends were bogged down and exhausted with second children. And everyone envied them and pitied them; how happy they seemed, she and her husband so lean and handsome, with his one lazy eye that seemed always just about to wink, and his stupid, stupid suntanned skin.

At first there was no real explanation and they lived with murky hope, which, thinks Mother now, is exactly the same as living with real dread, only more polite. They underwent all sorts of tests and passed and failed together with flying colours. Outside the fertility specialist's office was a sign that read PLEASE REMOVE RUBBERS, and they both laughed so hard they had to sit outside, doubled over on the icy steps. Inside the office, the grandfatherly doctor said the word *ejaculate* so many times, as both a noun and a verb, that they both crossed their legs and clutched each other's hands and imagined that it was just another one in a series of tests, this one to measure their maturity levels.

What Mother remembers thinking is that there must have been a seed of badness that none of the microscopes could detect, in both of them, but mainly in her, that kept them from bringing forth life. A badness in their love, in how much of it there really was, how much pleasure they could give each other, how much they still loved to look at and into each other after all these sad and disappointing years, in how strong they were. When all her friends began muttering under their perfidious breaths, rumblings of unhappiness that were as loud and painful as hunger, what could she say? That she was still in love with her husband. And just as she moved away a little, if only inside her pruney, shrivelled heart, from her more fecund friends, these same friends took a slight step backwards out of the glare of this marriage, which was almost like fluorescence it made everyone else look so ugly. But somehow, from all of this, Mother drew the conclusion that something about her love was bad and that some people couldn't have everything.

One night Eddie came home with a dog, a tiny pug, a pugilist of a dog with a blackened, punched-in face. He called him Og the Fertility Dog, and true to stereotype, the dog went everywhere with them and lay between them on the bed when they slept and at the foot of the bed, snorting, while they made love and prayed. They joked about him and called him the ugliest baby in the world, still they carried him around like a talisman. In the end, the only thing that happened was that Mother's ovaries got cystic, first one and then the other, in what she imagined was a kind of fizzing, the sound you might get if you experimented by pouring acid on something, and she imagined that all her hidden bitterness, her acerbic secret sadness, was causing her insides to burn and bubble. Several operations later, Mother was left with just a small piece of ovary – for what? thought Mother. As a memento, or a wishing penny at the bottom of a well. After a few more years they renamed the dog Ug the Pug, but he was there ten years later when their daughter came home from the hospital with them, sitting by the new bassinet, breathing heavily in his way that made him always sound as though he were underwater, snorkelling really, and then he died, miraculously one week later, his generative mission strangely accomplished.

When Mother remembers all this she thinks about photographs, how snapshots, like some realist paintings, are

technically good, sometimes even awesome in their repro-
duction of the real thing, but somehow empty too. Not lies
exactly, just silly stories, evidence for anecdotes. A family that
really wants to keep a record of itself should hire a photog-
rapher to go around snapping all the terrible and ironic
moments. Forget the silly zoo, the vacation poses, and the
beach, the beach, the endless beach. Instead, her album would
be filled with pictures of her and Eddie sitting together, hand
in hand, in all the various offices, while social workers ask
them strange and terrible questions about their sex lives and
banking habits, and doctors say things like "normal infertility" and "chemotherapy," and still they clutch each other's
hands exactly like kids on a roller-coaster ride. Just exactly.
And then maybe a photograph of her and her daughter, not
smiling, but after the smile, when she looked seriously at her
little baby and thought: I'm happy you are not from me
because I will never have to see myself in you. And finally, of
course, a photograph of her leaving her daughter's room just
the other night, after her first big lie, her face smug and
stunned and radiant. Hoo boy!

Just a few summers ago, the last summer her husband was
alive, they went to the beach, and while Eddie slept in his
lightweight jogging suit and baseball hat and her daughter
quite literally buried herself in the sand, Mother watched
an awful family, a shrewish mother and a bullying father,

setting up their beach chairs, stiff, upright plastic chairs that looked as though they'd been hauled away from a set of patio furniture. The parents sat bolt upright, facing the sun, while their boys huddled together under a small beach umbrella, taking turns digging with a plastic spoon. "Take off your sweatpants. What kind of idiots wear sweatpants at the beach," the mother said to her children. "No wonder you don't have any friends, neither of you," the father lev-elled at his boys, and then to the mother he hissed, "Everyone is laughing and playing in the water like real kids and these two are as startled and dumb as rabbits. I'm so happy," he said again to the children, "that you both could join us on our family vacation."

Frustrations, resentments, thick as the sea air, floated toward Mother. The gulls squawked and puffed about them in mimicry. Mother stared for a moment at her own child, her long, thin girl body flattened against the sand, covered in a striped towel, her cheek and temple pressed against a sand pillow, and thought how sadness made a mockery of our lives and all our best intentions. It was this, really: that her daugh-ter's moods filled her with self-loathing. How often she had wanted to yell at her own daughter, Get up, for goodness sake. This is my life too!

Then one of the sulky, overdressed boys began to cry and went off to sit by himself near the narrow green wooden fence in the dunes. The father got up quickly and ferreted through his plastic beach bag. Mother half-expected him to come up with a whip or a paddle but instead he emerged with a giant camera and an enormous lens. He stood in front of his miserable son, adjusting the focus manually, and said finally, "Smile!" And then horribly, "Just kidding." There, thought Mother. There was a terrible family who knew the true worth of a photograph and a real honest-to-goodness moment. Eddie had always been the picture taker in the family but this time the camera sat at the bottom of their canvas bag heavy as an anchor.

◗◗◗

"Come on up," says Will. "Come up and we'll chatter like widows." Will's wife left him years ago and he still likes to pretend that she is dead. "We split for financial reasons," Will told Mother when he first moved in. "I was poor and she was losing interest. Ba-doompa," he said, hitting his knees like a drum. Now, Will and Mother sit curled on his corduroy sofa, each of them snugly wrapped in ugly orange blankets that Will knitted himself. It is late October and cold and everyone is waiting until the very last second to turn on the heat. Her daughter is at a session with her therapist, someone Will recommended after Eddie died, someone he thought was good and kind and perfect because she seemed almost genderless. "She's a woman who looks a lot like a man but also a lot like a man who looks like a woman, if you know what I mean. Her hands are big, her feet are small, and her hair is neutral grey," Will said. "In other words, she doesn't look like a mother or a father, which in this case is a good thing."

Just last week her daughter came home from her appointment and said, "Dr. Dubois says that until I find my roots I will always feel somewhat formless."

"Yes," said Mother, evenly, faultlessly. "Yes, I guess she's probably right." Ah, Dubois, she thought. The kindness of strangers is always overwhelming. Each month Mother wrote a cheque to Dr. Babs Dubois, and each time as she pictured her, poised, moderate — let's face it, almost androidal (although lately as hot and wily as any other interloper, it seemed) — she thought for the millionth time, Babs? Babs? Honestly! Don't admit to that. Don't for heaven's sake put that name after the word *doctor*. But names, names have become everything. Names are the beginning and the end of the world.

"I just want to know her name," says her daughter. And, "Chances are I had another name, a birth name, the name she gave me." Before Eddie died, Mother remembers looking up the word *edelweiss* in the dictionary for a crossword she was doing, and just above she saw the word *eddy* and beside it, like a prophecy, its plural *-dies* and then its verb conjugations *-died* and *-dying*. And then Mother remembers lying in her big bed, months after Eddie died, her flannel nightgown prim and snug around her neck, riffing on her husband's name and thinking that even as his body was long gone from hers, his name was like a stump, something left over from a thing cut down, holding every nuance of his memory. She thought of him and rhymed out of sadness: Ed is dead. Eddie is deady. Edward went deadward.

Mother and Will hear the door to her apartment downstairs open and slam. "Hello?" she hears her daughter call, and Mother holds her breath for a second, nervous and cold as though she is playing hide-and-go-seek. Didn't she used to come through that door calling "Mom?" Didn't she?

"You know," Mother says to Will, "if Ed were here now he would look at her stricken face and bring her home a kitten." She laughs and then is surprised by her laughter and almost covers her mouth. She hadn't thought it was particularly true as she said it, but after she said it she realized it was all that was true, as though Eddie were pressing into her head from far above her with all his ideas and needs to fix things, to fill up all absences with quick, soft, substitute love: Og the Fertility Dog instead of their very own baby, a kitten instead of a mother, and, in the last few months of his life, another ridiculous pug for her, for company, that she named, lazily, Ug Two, Pug Too, and that right now she could hear click-clacking back and forth across her kitchen floor, following her daughter from the fridge to the sink and back again. Oh, she missed Eddie, especially when she was so cold, especially all the time, especially now when she so badly needed to be edified.

Mother uncurls her legs, her surprised body popping open its joints reluctantly, and is surprised to find that she does not make that "ouf" sound, the sigh that reminds her that the body always knows its age. In fact, today she is feeling almost limber; her head is steady, her knee isn't cramped. She points her toes straight out and feels a shiver beginning to spread up her body, as though she has just stepped from somewhere cold into somewhere hot. Her body flushes, a deep spreading blush that makes her tingle, vibrate almost, as though she's been caught in a draft – or does she mean lie? Or does she mean web, caught like a fly in a web of deceit?

If Will only knew, surely he would delight in pointing out that she was in fact the spider herself and not the hapless fly – still, she feels tangled, stunned as food, ambushed. The thing about webs, thinks Mother, is that no matter how much you slap at your head or flap your hands about, the sticky filaments settle upon you like shame, like just another layer of skin.

But how can she explain this sense of being ablaze, hot and alive with something? She hears her daughter downstairs as a kind of distant, muted kicking, as though her apartment below were her own surprising, pregnant stomach, full with thumping life. And of course it frightens her that her lies have become so invigorating, her lies that should be as heavy as pain are making her feel light as vapour.

Just last night she told another story. It was inexcusable, just horrendous, but she was giddy with recklessness and oh it was a doozy, and there was her daughter's face, gazing, for once in such a long time, fully at her, enraptured. For once, she had all the world, or something like it, to offer. "One time," she told her daughter, "when you were around seven, the phone rang in the middle of the night and when I picked it up, there was no one on the line, so I banged down. Then it rang again, and I was spooked, so I got your dad to answer it. He said, 'Hello? Who is this? What did you say? What did you say?' and then he put the phone down. I had never actually seen your father so tense and I was sure that he was about to tell me that someone had died, my mother, his father, I ran through all the possible dying people we knew in about two seconds. But what he said was that there had been breathing for a few seconds on the line and then a woman's voice, thick and raspy, said, 'I'm a friend of your daughter's,' and then dad said he heard some kind of shuffling in the background and the line disconnected. We stayed up all night, restlessly gripping each other's hands. We thought of calling the police and we watched you like a hawk for months, but soon the whole thing dropped from the tip of our minds like a bad dream."

It was unforgivable to use Eddie this way, to give the ghost all the best lines, to make the lie once removed because it was unverifiable. And anyway, thought Mother, it was true in a way, in the way that all experiences of the mind and imagination are true, and all she really forgot to say was, "A few nights ago I had this crazy dream. . . ." She had intended to but it just came out differently, it came out like a bedtime story, or better, a ghost story, and as though she were in a play and had merely bumbled a line, but she kept on going like a pro, improvising the lines as she went. "It's probably nothing," she told her daughter. "It's just that lately I have been thinking about that again, how strange it was, and sickening."

It was true that her instinct had never been towards the whole truth. It was Eddie who had always been the straight shooter and who saw things for what they were. Only her hope, before her daughter was born, kept her good, and, afterwards, it was always her fear that this too-good thing would be snatched back, stolen away, if she didn't keep her heart smooth and perfect, and her mind clear from anger. She started checking the doors and the windows at night and clicking down the locks of the car in neighbourhoods she knew were good and safe. She never shoved her daughter in frustration or grabbed her roughly with impatience. As far as she was concerned, there was always someone watching.

For instance, it was Mother who wondered, and not Eddie, what the purpose was of telling her daughter about her adoption. At the time, the newest books, the most conscientious, striving social workers, seemed to concur that honesty about the child's adoption was the best way to go. But Mother stood alone and had her doubts. What could she do? People were just starting to use the word "groovy" seriously. What a crock, thought Mother, what nerve, to imagine that half a story was better than no story at all, that one tiny thread of plot could substitute for all that was missing. Would it ever make any sense to tease her daughter with another life she would probably never have access to? All the world was steeped in covert operations, why the sudden burning need for total disclosure? Poor Mother. Older than most of the crowd, she had entirely skipped the summer of love and moved straight on to the summer of denials and cover-ups.

And what difference would it really make if her daughter never knew, if the wonder of that whole birth thing was kept just where it had always been for Mother, as a complete mystery. At least this they would have in common. Betrayals, secrets were nothing new. Plenty of relationships had survived secret affairs, one night indiscretions, and all the other details better left unsaid, hadn't they? Why wasn't it the same? "We will always look empty-handed to her," Mother told her husband. "Our throats will be full and choked with love, our hearts sick to overflowing, but our hands will always appear empty, and secret as fists." Because it was true that in their love for their daughter there was no difference. Mother has to stop herself sometimes from remembering a pregnancy that she never had.

The truth was that while her daughter was young, it hardly came up. Her daughter was shy, well mannered, afraid of so many things, and when she got angry she would bite and scratch at her own arms rather than hurt anything around her. She anthropomorphized everything. She apologized when she bumped into a table, she got teary when she saw an apple freezing in the snow, and wondered often where all the wild animals of the city went to die. Only sometimes, at night, to stall bedtime, would she say, "Tell me that story again . . ." And Mother would stay and tell, in a sing-song voice that sounded as though she were about to launch into a limerick, the story of her daughter's adoption. *Well,* she would begin, *there once was a woman who loved you very much but for some reason couldn't keep you, and we were so lucky that you came to live with us.* (The End, she hoped, she always hoped, in a broken-hearted way.) Was that ever enough of a story? wondered Mother. Or was it always only a little ditty, a mere jingly trailer for the real story to come, if it ever did?

It was such a smooth and practised piece, it sometimes felt to Mother that she was simply reciting a beloved nightly nursery rhyme, another, even more bizarre, version of "Peter, Peter, Pumpkin Eater." (We've kept you very well, she would think, alarmed again at her defensive, insistent thoughts. Look how very well we've kept you.)

"That's it?" her daughter would ask sometimes. "That's all you know?"

"That's all I know, angel," Mother would answer, smoothing down her daughter's fine, thin hair. And sometimes that seemed exactly true.

And then there was one time when her daughter was ten. Her daughter, the champion animal lover, was pleading again for a dog and so they took her to the shelter just to see what was there. She stopped in front of every cage and regarded the dogs seriously, her lips pressed flat together in what Mother thought was careful attention but later realized was some sort of sad recognition. She moved from cage to cage, concentrated and focussed, and never once reached her hand over to touch them. In the parking lot, she leaned into Mother and broke down in abandoned weeping, unashamed, maudlin sobbing. She was still filled with sweet, obvious, childish correlations. This was long before she became distant and ironic. But her question was already beginning to reveal signs of her future self, wounded and proud at the very same time. She asked simply: "Did you think you were saving *my* life?"

"Oh, God no," said Mother, shaking and pulling her daughter in to herself, rocking her back and forth in her arms, and pressing her so close to her cold fur coat that she imagined from far away she must look like a huge bear mauling a small child. "No," she repeated again. "I thought you were saving mine."

"You should never have said that to her," said Will, so many years later when Mother told him. "No wonder she is so careful around you, always asking your permission first before she tells you to fuck off."

●━●━●

In her small office at the bookstore, a cramped, converted closet actually, Mother skims through a new release called *No Regrets: Doing It All Now the Right Way*. She swore to Eddie that her shop would always be strictly intelligent and literary, eclectic, even a little precious, but never, never self-help. But, in the end, she caved in and of course they were good sellers, bestsellers often, and she compromised by knocking out a small supply closet at the back of the store, painting the walls an ugly deep rust, hanging extra bright spotlights, and exiling these books to this remote and cramped section of the store. Mother thought of it as the dirty-book room, like in those video stores where the X-rated section is through the squeaky swing doors. She reads now: *Mothers, what do you most need to tell your daughters today?* Mother closes the book quickly. She does not want to read their suggestions. Surely, they will say something about truth and love and make some sort of obvious word play on the two – the truth in love and the love of truth, that sort of thing. Instead, Mother looks down at her hands, turning them back and forth, still pleased that she has made it through most of her adult life without a manicure. Everyone agrees that she has beautiful hands, a little veiny and a bit too green in the wintertime, still, long delicate fingers that might have been good for hand-cream commercials or sign language. Mother knows people watch her hands when she talks, the way they punctuate her ideas with flourishes, and she knows it is hard to keep people's attention on her eyes. Her daughter, on the other hand, has boxy fingers and square nails, and her thumbs curl back in this odd, double-jointed way. Even her toes are strange, curled, prehensile, seem always to be clenched, and could grab at almost anything. "Scary," said Eddie the first time he saw her tricky hands and feet. All these years, Mother has been keeping her eye on the women who come in and out of her bookshop. She does it now by habit; she hardly knows what she is doing. In the winter she watches women pull off their thick mittens or gloves. In the summer, she finds herself staring down at their sandals. She does exist, after all, this woman. And she could be anywhere.

Mothers? What is it you most want to tell your daughters? Here is one true thing, thinks Mother absurdly. It is true that without a certain kind of nose, you will never be drop-dead beautiful.

Once, just after Eddie died, Mother was sitting in the dark living room wishing she had a habit, something to inhale, ingest, imbibe, inject, bite, or twirl, anything to distract her from the horrible fact that it was the first snow and Eddie's body was naked in the ground. She heard her daughter come in silently to watch her neat classic mother sitting, hands folded softly in her lap, grieving. "What is it," asked Mother, "that you will most remember about me when I am gone? In other words, have I taught you anything?" She hadn't particularly felt like speaking, she had this feeling that she could go on in silence forever, but she could feel her daughter needing to be drawn out of herself, could feel her distant and defensive daughter coming near. "Well," said her daughter, not moving, speaking straight out into the dark window and the first falling snow. "I learned to have a soft touch, to handle things with care, and to make all my gestures smooth and deliberate. I have never seen you squeeze anything. I have never seen you grab." Had her daughter really said that? Just like that, soft and evenly like a speech. How creepy, she'd thought, and she'd had an awful sinking feeling that her daughter had been silently practising another eulogy. "No really," said Mother. "Don't be flowery, just be straight." "Oh," said her daughter, already impatient, turning away again. "I'll just miss you, okay? You're my mother, aren't you?"

Here's something, she thinks, still skipping randomly through the book. *Write a letter to your loved ones and put it away in a special box of keepsakes. Say all that was unsaid. Forgive, forgive, and set everyone free with love.* Once, long ago, Mother heard a story about a woman whose husband had died but had left behind for his love to find in every single breast pocket of his empty, abandoned suits, a folded piece of paper upon which he had written only one lonesome, heart-stopping word: *Goodbye.* After Eddie died, Mother searched his room and all his belongings for just such a message but she found nothing. It was because, she realized, Eddie never left anything unsaid, and so his things, all his neatly ordered files, his immaculate desk drawer and old hat box filled with mementos from his youth that Mother had seen a million times, everything after he left, was silence. "When I am gone," said Eddie to her once, during a pause, a rest stop in between some really bad days, "I want to be really gone. The last thing I want to do is hang around and haunt you."

Here's the worst thing Mother ever said to Eddie. They were driving home from the hospital and Eddie was saying peculiar and unthinkable things. He was saying, I am going home to die now. I want to die at home. He was a tiny man now, so small Mother had been surprised to find that she had no problems at all lifting him from his wheelchair, cradling him against her, and placing him softly on the car seat without swinging or banging his legs. He was like one of those trick mugs, the ones that looked like heavy, thick glass, the ones you braced yourself to lift only to find that they were actually made of plastic. It reminded Mother of picking up a dying seabird once, surprised to find that up close this common bird seemed huge and yet in her arms he was so light. Certain things after that made a kind of sense to her; for instance the phrase "light as a feather" was more than just an expression. It was, in fact, something true. "Fine," said Mother. "That's just fine with me. But how about I smash the car right this second and then all our daughter will have to remember is this awful wreck? Or how about I tell her you died in the parking lot. Instead, I'll rent us a beautiful hotel room. I'll come and take care of you every day, just like that. Why should your little girl have to see this in her own house? How will we ever be able to live there without you after that?"

Awful. It was just awful. Unforgivable, and yet he had forgiven her. He was, by then, way past the point of pettiness. He could no longer be provoked. She remembers how serious she felt, not so much about the hotel room, but about smashing the car right there and then, into a lamppost or some oncoming car. Just to do it now and fast, if they had to do it at all. But then she thought of her daughter standing in the middle of their house like something hot at the core of the earth, surrounded on all sides by all of their things; mementos and souvenirs wherever she looked, enough knick-knacks to fill a lifetime of remembering.

Mother thinks of her daughter's original mother and thinks this: Stupid, stupid girl. Why couldn't she have left her daughter something? A letter, a glove, a piece of her stupid hair. Was she a moron? A simpleton? Probably a cruel and reckless beauty queen. Probably an impossibly loose bully. Look at all the lies she is pushing Mother to tell. It is as though Mother's own love is weak, watered down, muted, and she is being forced into speaking like a ventriloquist through the mouth of this dummy, dummy girl. Surely, thinks Mother, an idea tightening in her imagination, you were the type of person everyone followed behind, picking up the pieces. Suddenly she feels restless, perky almost, or maybe just spirited, and wonders for a moment if at her age it is too late to take up running.

Oh, house of terminal sadness, Mother says to herself as she comes through her front door. She bends down to pat Ug Two, who is snorting around her heels, his tongue and tail both curled in that same neat trick. From her daughter's room she can hear Jacques Brel sweating heavily through "Ne me quitte pas," and Mother wonders what, what in the world does this have to do with anything? And then she decides that maybe all of love's pain has to do with awful and embarrassing abandonment, but wouldn't it be sweet and easy if only her daughter were suffering from a silly boyfriend who was doing something simple and treatable, like breaking her heart. Mother picks up the pug and mouths the words to the song into his flat, gloomy face. If anything, thinks Mother, this is my song. Mine. Mine. Mine. She switches on some lights in the dark house and thinks that it was never supposed to be like this. She was supposed to have a huge family, children everywhere doing things like clamouring, and banging down the bathroom door, filling up her days with distractions, her whole house like a small old-fashioned school — each room for a child of a different grade. But never this. Never this quiet one-to-one faceoff, like two methodical, quiet chess players locked in their heads by their own strategies. Her house was spotless, immaculate. For once, thinks Mother, I'd like to come through the door and trip over something. Where is the rowdy cha-cha-cha of family life, she wonders. Where are the romps and jigs and good-natured pranks, the basic showy pageant of love between people. The seriousness of serious things is overwhelming, and it is not making her a better person. It is making her bad, very, very bad. And worst of all Mother cannot stop cracking egg jokes to herself. She thinks: We are walking on eggshells here. She thinks: I have put all my eggs in one basket.

On the kitchen table Mother finds two of her daughter's humiliations. The first is a failed chemistry test and the second is the Adoption Disclosure form that, because her daughter is a minor, needs the signature of a legal guardian. Oh, thinks Mother, sitting down suddenly at the table. The sadness of your children is much, much worse than your own. Say it ten times very fast.

❧

"Beware the elf in your self," says Will, and not for the first time. Mother wonders, also not for the first time, why she loves Will the way that she does when often he is so obvious and simple. He still cannot get over the coincidence of the rapist in therapist. To Will, etymology is another level of consciousness. He is going to a conference for a few days and Mother has promised to watch his cat, and right at this moment she is listening to him explain how she needs to thump the cat's rump vigorously while he is eating because he is old and skinny and needs constant encouragement at mealtimes. Will demonstrates and the cat goes very still, except for his tail which begins to swoosh spastically from side to side. The cat, thinks Mother, does not look encouraged, he looks as though he is braced for anything, he looks as though he is thinking instead: Life is startling, better eat fast. As usual, Mother is surprised and comforted by the kooky things people do in the privacy of their own lives.

Mother watches Will pack a small bag. He wraps his cologne in a Baggie and shoves it in a zippered side pocket. Mother sits in the centre of Will's bed feeling much younger than she is, and she plays a little game in her head where she pretends that she is Will's lover and he is leaving her. Will is sixteen years younger than Mother, that same magical number that is her daughter's prickly age. She doesn't want Will, so none of this fantasizing hurts her. Still, she is always flattered when, unprompted and just a little flirty, Will might say, "Look at you. You could do those Oil of Olay guess-my-age ads. Your genes are truly miraculous."

Forty was old to have a baby, and at forty, before they brought her daughter home, she felt old, but after that, once she'd held her first and only child, she never again felt any older. Eddie, who was six years older than she, worried more than she did. "When she's twenty, I'll be sixty-six. She'll be off to college and I'll be retiring." Once, even, Eddie had taken her out in the stroller and some woman had stopped him in the park and told him what a beautiful granddaughter he had. In a panic,

Eddie dyed his hair an ugly tar-black and took up playing squash, but after a few years or so he seemed reconciled to the age gap and comforted himself with the idea that he would be wise and distinguished way before any of the other parents.

Once, when their daughter was eleven, she shyly asked her mother if she could dress her for parent-teacher day. She made it sound jokey, playful, but underneath, Mother knew, her daughter's mind was serious and worried. She put Mother in a pale-blue and pink mohair sweater with a gigantic cowl neck, and a pair of tight brown wool pants, which she made her tuck into a pair of taupe, spike-heeled boots. She pinned back Mother's hair with two purple combs studded with rhinestones, and dangled a pair of multi-coloured enamelled earrings from Mother's recently pierced ears. Mother remembers the look in her eyes as her daughter stood back to survey her mother. She was trying to see her as others might, as an older woman who was still beautiful, an older woman who looked as young as anyone else. "You look great, mom," her daughter actually sighed. "Just great for over half a century," and she smiled and hugged her, and there was nothing strange between them, just this game they both knew they were playing. All day long through the school, Mother click-clacked and wobbled in her high boots. She chit-chatted with the other mothers with extra vigour. She leaned on one hip with her hand in her back pocket. Her daughter beamed and beamed and never let go of her other hand.

Mother sees suddenly that if her daughter finds this woman, she will be much, much younger than Mother. Younger than Will even, a girlfriend for Will. Her daughter would never have to dress her up, she could say simply, My mother is so young. And no longer, My mother looks so young for her age. Well, thinks Mother. She might even be young enough to be my own daughter; maybe I am the same age as this woman's own mother. Mother toys with all these different ages, counting years forwards and backwards, tapping her fingers quickly against her thigh to help her keep track. I don't want any of this, she thinks. No not at all.

●━●━●

Mother sits in Will's apartment. The cat sits on her lap purring in an almost chokey, disgruntled way. He has lost most of the hair on his belly and he presses against her knitted sweatpants for warmth. She is using Will's ancient typewriter, a clunky manual, cranky and stubborn as a goat, the ribbon so faded she is typing almost in grey. Yesterday, at a crummy flea market, she bought an old wooden box decorated with small, fading pink hearts. She bought a round gold metal that said FOR EXCELLENCE IN MATHEMATICS, and the seller assured her it was more than twenty years old. She bought an old picture frame and a tattered book of poems by Whitman. She tore out the first few lines from "Song of Myself" and put it behind the glass frame:

I celebrate myself, and sing myself,
And what I assume you shall assume,
For every atom belonging to me as good as belongs
    to you.

I loaf and invite my soul. . . .

She bought a tiny bracelet, a child's bracelet ringed with charms, and put it in the box. She thought of using an old photograph of a young girl sitting in a park that she had seen at one of the stalls, but could not bring herself to go that far, could not really face what she was doing and put a face to it. She typed:

Dear Artemis,
    I am so sorry and I wish you everything you would wish for yourself. There is nothing I can give as an explanation except to say that the timing is awful and I never wanted to hurt anyone. I have plans for myself, a life to begin and my studies to consider. I leave you a few of my treasures but you will need the rest of your life to find your own. I read a mythology book and Artemis was the name of the goddess of the hunt, the

forest, and the animals. Please be strong and please, please don't try and find me. Nobody knows about you and I couldn't bear to be found out.

I will think of you.

It is clear that Mother has thrown caution and everything credible to the wind. She throws her daughter to the wind, and at the same time she gives herself away. Artemis? Now what is that all about, what is she thinking anyway? Is there a soul alive who could find any of this believable? The question is, does her daughter have the jeweller's talent for gripping the magnifying loupe against her sharp, clenched eye, for telling the difference between a fake and the real thing? Does Mother choose this name and all its mythological hogwash because it reminds her of virgins who will not be claimed, who know how to put up the feisty, pure fight? Or is it because of the way it ripples through her mind and sounds instead just like artifice, like art, like arts-and-crafty?

It is clear to Mother that she is testing her own daughter against herself, and only a real mother could ever hope to be the loser. See through me, thinks Mother. Beat me. Know me. God, she thinks, don't let her fall for just anyone.

Mother's head throbs from not breathing and she exhales so loudly the cat is startled and jumps off her lap, catching a claw in the wool of her pants. She speaks out loud to Will's empty apartment, part question, part confession. Will I do this terrible thing? Will I? For so long now she has felt that she was being watched but who knew who was watching? For her, life in a way had been so much more frightening before she knew anyone who had died, before she loved with all of her strength someone who was dead. Before, who knew who was up there? Now it is different. Now, she feels it is Eddie who is watching her, and Eddie loves her and would forgive her anything. Even this.

Just this morning her daughter was tinkering around with the word *death*, puttering with her cruel little sharp tools. Conjugating it like a lesson: *I want to die. I wish I were dead.* And the mother of them all: *I wish I had never been born.* You felt two ways with children; maybe you always did. I mean, thinks Mother, one can always feel two things at once about one's own. Everybody wants to feel that they are good, good, good. How can you not hate for one minute anyone who makes you feel bad? She wants to shake her daughter by the shoulders, back and forth, back and forth, and she imagines how she would feel in her tight hands: soft and stuffed and dumb, her head flopping like a balled-up sock. She wants to shout her daughter's pissy face open: What difference does it make who you came from, where you came from? And at the same time

she wants to thrust her hand inside her daughter's body like
a demented and powerful healer, grabbing all the coiled and
crimped threads of her daughter's being, unravelling, unravelling the helix of all her years, her whole long life moving
backwards in fast motion like a film in reverse, until Mother,
the benevolent and all-seeing angel, grabs the egg that became
her daughter between her gorgeous fingers, and squeezes it like
an oily bath bead until it is nothing.

Mother folds the letter and closes the box. She thinks of
her daughter and imagines her sad and gullible. In a way, she
envies her daughter, free and unattached. Mother would like
to be that way but instead she is thinking, I held you, I stayed
up with you, I cooled your fevers and changed you. I listened
to everything you had to say. I cooked for you and fed you
by hand. I held you when you cried. You were so light I could
lift you and hold you on my lap. It occurs to Mother suddenly that she no longer knows who she is talking to, Eddie
or her daughter. Loss, as a substance, is something thick. It
pulls at her hair like wax. One hurt melts into another. She
remembers her daughter's arms gripped around her knees,
tugging down her pants so that they hung uncomfortably at
her hips, sobbing into her pant legs in the kindergarten corridor: Don't go, please. And how she'd bent her big body
down to peel her daughter's limbs away, section by section
like a fruit, until her daughter was just skin on the floor, and
she said firmly, she actually said as though life were in fact

impossibly long and there would be years and years to make up for everything: I am saying goodbye now, dear. You'll be fine. Because that is what the kindergarten teacher told her to say.

So Mother breathes deep and readies herself for her biggest lie yet. No one is telling her what to say now and so she thinks freely what she has always really believed: that the idea of the truth is always better than the truth itself.

◉◉◉

"Come," she says to her daughter, "Walk with me." She is giving her one last chance. She is looking for a way out. She plays games with herself. If she takes my hand, thinks Mother, I will not give her the box. If she leans into me and says something nice, I will not give her the box. But they walk side by side, not touching, their footsteps muffled by the covering of thick, wet leaves. The little dog hops along beside them, stopping at every bare tree, lifting his back leg as high as he can so that he is practically doing a handstand. Mother is wearing Eddie's old rain boots and a long black coat he used to call his slicker. Her daughter is wearing an old zipperless leather jacket that she found in a neighbour's garbage, and she wraps her arms around her chest to keep it closed. Mother thinks, I will not tell her to wear a hat. I will not ask her where her scarf is. When I speak next, it will be only through the flat, painted mouth of the dummy mother, that puppet mouth that opens to show a huge hole that goes nowhere.

Here's what Mother knows. She knows that from now on until some undisclosed time in the future, her daughter will always be slightly withdrawn. Mother has friends who have daughters and she has heard them say at different times: You look lovely today, mom. Or: Did you get your hair done? It looks great. Some have children who are already calling them "dear," calling them every day and calling them sweet names. Of course, most of her friends' children are grown, some even with children of their own. Still, last year a friend was in the hospital, and Mother watched a dutiful daughter support-ing her mother's grey, heavy head for a sip of water, smooth-ing ice chips over her cracked lips, emptying her spit cup, even massaging her swollen, lumpy feet. Mother cannot ever imagine her own daughter reaching out to touch any part of her bare body. It seems now, to her, that everything she will say from this time on will always sound unreal, theatrical, as impossible and beautiful as fiction. For instance, right at this moment, while they are walking like this, she could say: Remember when you got your tonsils out and the beautiful nurse let you brush her long red hair? Or she could say: Your dad and I were lovers until the very last moment. Or: Are you still afraid of thunder? Remember how you would tremble? How had this happened to them, that every word between them became so heavy and precious that speaking filled them with self-consciousness and they were stilted and phony as actors. And what was left after that? Curtain calls and, if she was lucky, occasional lunches.

It was the end of something, and endings were always like this, sloppy, abrupt, tactless. Even with Eddie, Mother found herself enduring these long, horrifying silences, so long sometimes she would find herself checking for the movement of his chest. The past and the future were both off limits, out on the outer limits of hope and a better time. The only tense was the now, and what could they say? *It's warm in here. It's cold in here. Do you think you could hold down some soup?*

They are walking home now, having circled the block, and still her daughter has given her nothing. It is the waiting, thinks Mother, that is the hardest part. In the end what she wanted was for Eddie to die already or to get up and live the way he was before, and she wanted both at the same time. And now she thinks about her daughter: Do I want to hurt her or make her better? And again she thinks, both. She wants both.

That night Mother gives her daughter the box of keepsakes, although in some part of her mind she refers to it as the tinderbox, filled with dangerous, flammable dust. She says this: "They told me I had to wait until you were eighteen, but I see now that that will probably be too late, and anyway, what difference could it make? The social worker left it with me and told me to use my best judgement. I'll be here all night if you want to talk." Her daughter takes the box and Mother's hands are shaking so hard, her daughter, for just one second, actually looks concerned. Mother feels giddy and tries to think of Eddie to keep herself from laughing. She watches her daughter walk away like Miss America, clutching the box to her chest like a bouquet.

Mother hums, cooks eggs, burns them, and spends the rest of the night scraping the bottom of the pan with a knife, the high-pitched grating consuming every bit of her, and she imagines that what she is actually doing is sanding down her brain. The kitchen is dark and she works only by the little stove light. Finally, it is very late and she picks up the pug and carries him to her bedroom. She realizes her daughter will probably not come and talk tonight. And if she does, thinks Mother, I will have the lights off in the bedroom. She will never see my face. But while Mother is taking off her clothes and changing into her thin, worn nightgown, the door opens suddenly and her daughter is standing there. Mother does not have time to pull the nightgown over her face and so instead she presses it fast to her chest and holds it like a bath towel. Her daughter looks quickly down at the floor and says, "I don't believe this. Not one word of this. Everybody wants to be found out. That's just the way people are."

In bed now, Mother closes her eyes and thinks how she and Eddie thought love could conquer everything, and in the end how wrong they were. It was, of course, powerless against so many things — disease, death, longing. Mother lies still and thinks about the word *conquer* and realizes that, finally, even if love isn't victorious, it can still take pretty much anything it wants by force.

Here's what Mother thinks about as sleep comes to her, comes to her while she is breathing in and out as an entirely different mother, a mother who is up to her eyeballs in tricks and secrets. Here's what I'll do, she thinks, pressing her fingers deep into her eye sockets, making stars. I'll hire someone to be her mother. I'll rent an office and puff cigar smoke around it. I'll audition women to play the hardest role they've ever played. Whoever it is will have to get it just right, no amateurs, no one with soap-opera makeup. I'll write the script and make them say over and over again into my smug face: At last. Oh, honey. Can I touch you? I will stare these women down with my hard, hard eyes and my ungiving mouth and they will repeat, without stopping, until I find the perfect one: *I love you . . . I love you . . . I love you.*

ACKNOWLEDGEMENTS

What a rare privilege it is and how satisfying to be able to publicly acknowledge and thank many of the people to whom I owe my gratitude.

So, thank you —

To the teachers: L. Silverstein, F. Davis, G. Geddes, A. Mattison, E. L. Doctorow, and especially Lucy Rosenthal, for her support, encouragement, and friendship beyond all reason.

To the Canada Council and the Canada Council Explorations Program, for financial assistance during the writing of this book.

To Ellen Seligman, for her belief and commitment, editorial acuity, and, of course, for turning the imagined into reality. And to Lisan Jutras, for her attentive and always perceptive copy-editing.

To dear friends who kept reminding me of what exactly I was doing here: Lauren Schaffer, who showed by example what it meant to be committed to the work, and especially Rebecca Posner and her family, who seem to have always been there right from the beginning, from the very first written word.

To my parents for their complete and constant faith in me, their encouragement, their unwavering love and support, and their generous endowments.

And especially to Allan for balance and strength, sustenance and patience, love and everything else.

And finally, to *Family: Real and imagined. Present and absent. The idea of it and the thing itself.*